# "You've guessed what I'm going to ask?"

Jason's strange eyes held Sara. "I haven't the least idea," she said.

"Well, I'll have to spell it out for you, then. I want you to lay off my young brother."

Sara gasped at the gall of this near stranger. "You want me to...."

"I'm certainly not going to see my brother put at risk for a little bit of dangerous nonsense like you, my girl."

Sara managed to control her voice despite her rage. "You really take liberties," she said. "I intend to tell my stepfather exactly what you've said."

"He should be pleased," Jason replied. "He has bigger game in his sights for you than my poor brother...."

Despite Jason's handsomeness, Sara felt she had never before detested anyone so instantly and so thoroughly!

# MARJORIE LEWTY
is also the author of these
## *Harlequin Romances*

and this
## *Harlequin Presents*

# Prisoner in Paradise

by

MARJORIE LEWTY

*Harlequin Books*

TORONTO • LONDON • LOS ANGELES • AMSTERDAM
SYDNEY • HAMBURG • PARIS • STOCKHOLM • ATHENS • TOKYO

Original hardcover edition published in 1980
by Mills & Boon Limited

ISBN 0-373-02382-0

Harlequin edition published January 1981

# CHAPTER ONE

FROM where they sat beside the hotel pool, in the shade of the thatched *palapa* the whole breathtaking sweep of Acapulco Bay lay spread out below, under a deep blue sky innocent of a single cloud. The Mexican sun poured down as if it had never stopped shining and never would, and between the feathery fronds of palm trees lay the crescent of pale sand, broken only by the dark heaps of rock here and there. Beyond the sand the sea was sapphire, dotted by sails that made splashes of bright colour against the blue, and streaked with the creamy wake of speedboats, each with its tiny, doll-like figure leaning back at the end of the tow-rope. Everything smelled of heat and sea and the expensive fragrance of sprays and lotions that wafted on the late afternoon air of one of the world's most famous jet-set playgrounds.

The after-lunch siesta in the air-conditioned rooms of the great white honeycomb of a hotel was over and guests were beginning to drift out, bronze bodies clad in bikinis or shorts according to sex, to swim or ski or skin-dive or parachute-sail, or simply to lie in the sun like lizards until it was time to think about what to wear for dinner and which club or disco to visit afterwards.

The young man with the soft brown hair and boyish complexion propped himself on one elbow to gaze at the girl in the lounger beside him. 'Paradise must be like this—paradise, complete with angel. I don't ask for a whole troupe of angels, I only need one, and her name is Sara.' He spoke teasingly, but the blue eyes in his frank, ingenuous face were ardent, almost bemused.

The girl turned her head, dislodging the enormous round straw hat which was resting against the back of the chair behind her, its stiff brim propped against her delightful small nose. 'I don't think I really fancy being an angel just yet, Tim, but thank you all the same. You do say the nicest things,' She rescued the hat and dropped it beside her on the pale green pool-surround.

In this place, where lovely girls were everywhere, Sara Tildesley was more than ordinarily lovely. In the miniscule white bikini her slender body was evenly baked, by months of following the sun, to a silky biscuit colour. Her hair, drawn back from an appealingly fragile small face, was a glimmer of freshly-minted gold. But it was her eyes that were her most unforgettable feature. Enormous and deep-set behind thick curving lashes, they were a pure deep violet. She was just eighteen.

'I wish I were a poet, then I could think of even nicer things.' The boy leaned over and took one of the slim brown hands, playing caressingly with the fingers one by one, but after a moment Sara drew her hand away, glancing over her shoulder towards the hotel.

'It's all right, Sara, your stepfather's not around,' Tim Knight said. 'I saw him with the oil tycoon bloke and his pals when I was coming out just now.'

Sara's delicately arched brows drew together in a small frown. Ralph Francis, her stepfather, had been playing poker with that man Sorano more and more in the last few days and she had an idea that he had been losing money. Not that he had said so, and, of course, she really had no idea how much he could afford to lose. But she thought she had noticed a slight difference in him. He seemed less genial and urbane, more on edge, although he was still as charming and thoughtful as ever to her.

Tim was talking again and she turned her attention to

him. 'I get the idea that he doesn't seem to like us being together, Sara—d'you know why? Has he got anything against me?'

She said, rather too quickly, 'Of course not, how could he have anything against you? He doesn't know you.'

'I just thought he seemed to freeze up rather when he met us coming up from the beach this morning.'

'You're imagining it, Tim.'

But of course he wasn't, she knew that. Her stepfather certainly hadn't encouraged the numerous young men who had hovered round her since that day, almost a year ago, when he had taken her away from boarding school to be his companion, to share his life. There had been Toby Barnes in Monaco, and that nice young solicitor she had become friendly with in Grand Bahama, and one or two others who hadn't lasted as long as those two, even. As soon as they showed signs of becoming serious Ralph had warned them off. She never knew what he said to them, but whatever it was it had been effective. Ralph had a way of making people do what he wanted—not by force but by gentle persuasion, by taking acquiescence for granted.

He had used the same method on her, too, quite blatantly, and she hadn't minded. She'd been amused and even touched because she knew that it was because he wanted to have her with him. 'You don't want to bother with that young cub, my sweet,' he would tell her with his crooked, lazy smile. 'He's rather juvenile, isn't he? And I've no intention of losing you yet to any man. We're having fun together, aren't we?'

It *had* been fun, she assured herself; it had been marvellous, and Ralph had been marvellous to her. True, he hadn't bothered himself with her all the years she had been at boarding school, since her mother died when she was seven. Ralph led a sophisticated life and admitted

frankly that children didn't appeal to him. But he had
made up for it since. She remembered the day he had
turned up at her school in Dorset, handsome and charming and prosperous. They had talked together in the
study she shared with another girl, and he had looked
hard and thoughtfully at the seventeen-year-old in her
white blouse and grey skirt, her golden hair tied back
and her great violet eyes regarding him with shy interest.

'My God, Sara,' he'd said at last, 'you've turned into a
beauty and no mistake! We'll have to get you out of this
stuffy school, it's no place for you.'

And when the headmistress had come in he had announced, rather to her disapproval, that Sara would be
leaving at the end of the term and would, in future,
make her life with him.

The other girls had been thrilled. 'Golly, I wish I had
a stepfather like that, he's a smasher!' And 'Straight off
for a holiday in Monaco while we struggle with A-levels
—what do you know? Some people have all the luck!
What does he *do*, Sal? Is he a tycoon or just an ordinary
common-or-garden millionaire?'

They had all giggled at that, but now, nearly a year
later, Sara knew that she still couldn't answer that
question. If being a tycoon was having an office and
interviewing important business men, then Ralph certainly wasn't one. Perhaps he was a millionaire? That
seemed more likely. Certainly they had moved from one
luxury hotel to another in the past months. Monaco—
Italy—the French Riviera—the Costa del Sol—the
Bahamas—and now Mexico!

Ralph was popular wherever he went. He made
friends easily, played golf and tennis superbly well,
joined parties at the casinos. He bought Sara lovely
clothes and drew her into the circle of new acquaintances everywhere they went. After the years at boarding

school she enjoyed it all—what girl wouldn't? The luxurious hotels—the new grown-up clothes—the freedom—
the admiration. The one thing that troubled her was that
they never seemed to make any real friends. Acquaintances—yes. But as soon as they were beginning to get to
know people Ralph would whisk her away.

'We're leaving today, my sweet. This place becomes a
bore,' he would announce, and suddenly they were moving off to the next jet-set resort, and she had to begin all
over again to adjust to a new set of people. And always
the men her father introduced her to were men in his
own age-group, men in their forties and fifties. Whe-
never a young man began to take an interest in her he
was warned off. She hadn't really minded much. She
hadn't fallen in love with any of them and it was quite
flattering, she had thought, that Ralph shouldn't want to
lose her so soon.

But Tim was different. Tim was a darling and she was
going to miss him dreadfully when he left at the end of
the week. She had felt quite upset when Ralph had said,
over lunch, 'You don't think you're seeing too much of
the young Knight lad, do you, Sara love? He's a bit wet
behind the ears, don't you think?'

He had accompanied the words with his crooked, con-
fidential smile, as if she couldn't fail to agree with him.
But this time she had said, 'I like Tim, and I'm sure you
would too, if you really knew him. Couldn't you—
couldn't we ask him to have dinner with us tonight?
We'd have to invite his brother too, I suppose. He's leaving tomorrow—the brother, I mean—but Tim is staying
on until the weekend.'

'Sorry, love,' Ralph had said, gently regretful. 'I've
promised we shall dine with the Albertos and Carlos Sorano.'

'Carlos Sorano?' She pulled a face at that.

Ralph laughed. 'What's wrong with Carlos—you like him, don't you?'

'Not much,' she admitted, and wriggled her shoulders fastidiously, 'I don't like the way he looks at me.'

Her stepfather roared with laughter. 'That's the Spanish blood in him, my pet. They show their admiration in no uncertain way when there's a beautiful girl around. And after all'—he stroked her shining gold hair with pride—'you *are* the most beautiful girl in the hotel.'

'Flatterer!' she laughed back. But her heart sank at the prospect of having to spend another evening in the company of the heavily-built oil tycoon with the red moist lips and the thinning hair.

'Not flattery, my child, the truth! And Carlos likes you. You've made quite an impression there.' There was a glow of satisfaction in Ralph's handsome face which she found puzzling, for why should he be so very pleased that she had made an impression on Carlos Sorano? She had shrugged it way, telling herself that perhaps Ralph wanted to do business with the man in some way. But out here in the hot sunshine, with Tim Knight, she suddenly remembered the feeling she had had, as if something unpleasant were suddenly hanging over her, and she shivered.

Tim was gazing at her raptly. He took her hand again. 'I—there's something I must say to you, Sara.' He stopped, frowning desperately. 'Gosh, this isn't as easy as I thought.' He swung his legs off the lounger and turned to face her, leaning forward towards her. He swallowed. 'The fact is, Sara darling, that I've fallen most terribly in love with you.'

Oh no! she thought immediately. He's going to be hurt and I can't bear it—not Tim, he's too nice. She said gently, not smiling, 'But Tim, we've only known each other a few days.'

'Days—weeks—years—what does it matter?' he blurted out. 'Oh, I've fallen for girls before, or thought I had. I've even imagined I was in love. That's how I'm absolutely sure that with you it's different, totally different. It's not just because you're pretty and sweet and fun to be with. It's—oh, it's deep here, inside me.' He punched his smooth brown chest with a gesture that was absurd yet somehow touching.

'Tim, I—' she broke in rather helplessly.

But he was not to be stopped. 'You've got to believe me, Sara. I know I fool around and put on an act, but then everyone does in a place like this. You're supposed to be sophisticated and with-it and never to be serious about anything. You're one of the jet-set or the gilded group, or whatever you like to call it. But inside I'm miserable as hell, Sara, because I've got to leave in two days and I'm terrified I'll never see you again.'

Sara's great violet eyes were clouded. 'Tim, I'm so dreadfully sorry, but I can't see how—'

'Don't say it,' he pleaded. 'Don't turn me down flat. Just promise that we'll keep in touch somehow when I get back to Dorset.'

'Dorset?' she exclaimed. 'You never told me you lived in Dorset.' She made her voice pleased, interested, as if they were having an ordinary talk. Somehow she must defuse the situation and not let Tim hope for the impossible. 'I know Dorset well, I grew up there. I went to school not far from Bournemouth.'

'Gosh, did you? What a coincidence!' The blue eyes flashed with eagerness. 'No, not a coincidence—it must be meant to be. You know—Fate and all that!'

Far from defusing the situation she seemed to have made it even more critical. Tim was bubbling with enthusiasm now. 'Look, darling, couldn't we be engaged!' He looked away from her surprised face and hurried on,

'Not to tell anyone yet, if you didn't want to, because I expect they'd all say we were too young. But just between ourselves—so that we'd know, and——'

'Oh, Tim, stop it!' She was half laughing now. 'You're taking my breath away.' She sat up on the canvas lounger, hugging her slim knees. 'Thank you for asking me, Tim, it's awfully sweet of you, but I couldn't. You see, I'm not in love with you——' She saw the devastated look that came into his eyes and added quickly—'I've never been in love with anyone. Not really in love. Oh, pop stars and film actors—the usual ones all the girls at school fell for. But I've never had the chance to know any boys of my own age. I don't remember having a real home; my mother died when I was little and I've lived at boarding school since then until last year. Sometimes I visited school friends in the holidays, but their brothers were all younger—prep school age.' She chuckled, inviting him to see the joke as she added ruefully, 'I'm afraid I've lived a very sheltered life.'

But Tim didn't smile. He seemed to be thinking of something else to say that would convince her. His forehead was creased anxiously. 'You *do* like me, Sara? You don't—don't shrink away when I touch you?'

She squeezed his hand. 'Of course not, silly!'

'And you enjoy it when I kiss you?' he urged.

'Mm'm.' She nodded, eyes sparkling.

He leaned over and put his mouth against hers, tenderly, lingeringly, in a youthful, experimental kiss. Then he drew away and smiled into her eyes. 'There, how was that?'

'Lovely!' smiled Sara truthfully, and saw with a pang that he was trembling.

He searched her face and then sat back. 'That'll do fine to start with. The rest will follow—we'll have all the rest of our lives together. I'm sure, I've got a feeling about it.'

Then his head turned and he stared over her shoulder. 'Blast!' he muttered. 'Here's Big Brother, no doubt to get my nose back to the grindstone. He never fails to remind me when there's work to be done.' He pulled a face.

Sara glanced round and saw Jason Knight approaching them from the other end of the pool. She had only encountered Tim's elder brother a couple of times, in a group, and had thought he seemed rather abrupt and arrogant and not a bit like Tim. Tim had explained to her that they were here on a business trip combined with a holiday. He, Tim, had just finished at Cambridge and was being introduced into his niche as a junior member of the family firm which was, he said vaguely, something to do with boats—she hadn't quite gathered what. He was, he admitted, rather bored with the whole thing, but he supposed he would have to buckle down to it sooner or later.

Jason Knight came up now and stood looming over them. All the other men out here wore only swimming trunks as a matter of course, but this man had on canvas shorts and a shirt—a faded blue cotton affair which clung limply to his powerful shoulders and hung open to show a wide, muscular chest with a mat of dark hair.

Sara found herself resenting him—the tall, broad arrogance of the man, the faintly cynical twist of his mouth as he stood surveying them unsmilingly. He was horribly conceited, she was sure, and much too pleased with himself. She disliked him heartily before he even spoke, which was rare for Sara because she was a fair-minded girl who didn't normally make snap judgments on people she met.

He ignored her and spoke—rather brusquely, she thought—to his brother. 'I've finished my part now, Tim, and you can get cracking on the order sheets. You'll find all the gen on the table in the bedroom and you'd better make a start now. There's a fair amount to get through and I want to go over it with you before I leave in the morning.'

Tim grimaced towards Sara and pulled himself to his feet. 'Duty calls, I must obey.' He leaned down and brushed her hair with his lips. 'Don't forget, sweetheart,' he breathed into her ear, and strode away towards the hotel.

Sara expected that his brother would follow him, but instead he lowered himself into the lounger that Tim had vacated. He sat sideways on it, feet apart, hands clasped loosely between his knees.

'I'd like a word with you, Miss Tildesley,' he said in his deep, curt voice. His eyes moved over her in a way that, for some abrud reason, made the blood rise in a hot wave into her cheeks. No girl in Acapulco would think of wearing anything more than a bikini in the daytime, but this man somehow managed to turn his scrutiny of her near-nakendness into a subtle insult.

She reached down and picked up her enormous Mexican straw hat and held it in front of her. She would have preferred to sit up straight, feet on the ground, to face this man, but the two lounger chairs were pulled close and if she had swung round she would inevitably have brushed against his legs, which for some reason was quite unthinkable. So she hugged the hat before her knees and stared coolly at him. She couldn't imagine what he had to say to her, but whatever it was, his manner proclaimed that it wasn't anything particularly pleasant.

He met her gaze steadily. In the shade of the *palapa*

his eyes were a curious blend of grey and green—a kind of clay colour, with darker rims to the irises. Strange, almost hypnotic eyes.

He said, 'I dare say you've guessed what I'm going to ask you?'

She shook her head. 'I haven't the least idea.'

'No?' The long mouth pulled sceptically. 'Well, I'll have to spell it out for you, then. I want you to lay off my young brother.'

Sara gasped, hardly believing what she had heard. 'You—want—me—to——'

The broad shoulders under the faded blue shirt moved impatiently. 'Look, don't let's waste time. I'm a busy man and I've got a lot of work to get through this evening.'

'Then perhaps you'd better go and get on with it,' she said, anger rising hotly in her. The sheer gall of the man, thinking he could issue orders like that! 'I'm quite sure this conversation has gone far enough.'

She moved away, intending to wriggle off the chair, but his hand shot out and gripped her wrist, holding her painfully. 'Let me *go*!' she breathed furiously, with a covert look around at the people passing by. 'Let me go or I'll——'

'You'll what? Scream?' He lifted dark, mocking brows. 'They'd think it was a new game. Anything goes in Acapulco.'

Inside she was seething, but she kept her voice steady because he was probably right. 'Very well,' she said. 'Take your hand off me and I'll listen to what you have to say.'

He regarded her dubiously for a moment and then released her. Under his gaze she was horribly conscious that her breasts were rising and falling rapidly beneath the narrow strip of nylon that comprised the top of her bikini, which wasn't surprising because she was angrier than she had ever been in her life.

Her agitation hadn't escaped him—she got the feeling that nothing would escape this man—for he said with a faint smile that didn't reach his eyes, 'Don't alarm yourself, Miss Tildesley. I've nothing personal against you. In fact'—his tone became an insolent drawl as his eyes rested on her swelling bra—'I'm sure that in different circumstances we should get along very well together. But that's not at issue now. What *is* at issue is that my susceptible young brother appears to have got himself enmeshed in your—er—charms, and I've absolutely no intention of letting him make an idiot of himself.'

She stared at him, utterly transfixed. Her throat muscles felt rigid, but she made a tremendous effort and forced out between her teeth, 'Mr Knight, I find you offensive and insulting, and I must ask you to leave me.'

The words sounded like something out of a Victorian melodrama; she realised it as soon as they were out, and she expected him to laugh in that nasty, sneering way of his, but all she saw was a flicker of something that looked like surprise in the curiously coloured eyes as he sighed and said, 'Oh dear, you're going to be difficult and act the injured innocent. I assure you, Miss Tildesley, that won't work with me. It might stir young Tim's starry-eyed chivalry, but I've had time to see more of this wicked world than he has, and I feel responsible for him.'

'*Responsible?*' Her voice rose unsteadily. 'That's ridiculous! Tim's grown up. He's twenty-two, he told me so.'

'Responsible,' he repeated grimly. 'I brought him here and we're a long way from home and I've looked after Tim since he was a baby. I'm not going to say that I feel like a father to him, but I'm certainly not going to see all my good work put at risk for a little bit of dangerous nonsense like you, my girl.'

She couldn't stay sitting down and listening to this any longer. She slid off the lounger on the opposite side to him and stood up. 'For Tim's sake,' she said icily, 'and because you're his brother, I won't say all I'd like to say. Merely that I consider you ill-bred and utterly disgusting and——'

She stopped, her eyes widening. He had got up and stepped easily across the lounger to stand in front of her, thus cutting off her retreat, for the chairs were pulled into a corner close to the wall of the pool bar. He towered above her and she felt a cold trickle of fear run through her as she became aware of his sheer masculine strength. His arms and legs had the whipcord appearance of a man who spends most of his time out of doors and for all his size there was a leanness that spoke of superb physical fitness. A thought flashed through her mind that a woman wouldn't have a chance against a man like this, and she pushed it away again. She couldn't be in any danger from him in this sun-bathed pleasure spot.

She drew herself up and stared straight ahead. He was standing close—much too close, she thought faintly —and all she could see was the brown width of chest where his shirt hung open. 'Please let me pass,' she said stiffly. 'I shall go in and tell my stepfather exactly what's happened.'

From above her head his voice came with hateful confidence. 'Your stepfather won't be interested, I assure you. In fact, he'll probably be grateful to me for warning you off Tim. From what I've learned about the position I gather that he has altogether bigger game in his sights.'

By now Sara was so shattered by this whole horrid

episode that she was only partly taking in what he said. 'How—how dare you?' she faltered, close to treacherous tears.

He took a step back, reached into the hip pocket of his canvas shorts and pulled out a folded piece of paper. 'I took the precaution of bringing this with me,' he said with a grim smile. 'I thought it might help you to see sweet reason.' He put the paper into her hand. 'And for favours received.'

Taken by surprise, she unfolded the slip and looked down at it. It was a cheque for fifty pounds. 'You—you —of all the——' Words were choking her, forced out by a surge of fury such as she had never experienced before. With shaking hands she ripped the cheque across and flung it away from her. It landed on the canvas chair and the signature *Jason Knight*, in a bold black hand, seemed to stare up at her mockingly.

'Tut, tut, a little theatrical, surely?'

The contempt in his voice was the final straw. Adrenalin was flowing strongly in her and every part of her body was boiling with energy. She lifted her hand and struck him as hard as she could across his smiling mouth. Then she pushed past him and tore up the path to the hotel, brushing against the masses of fuchsia and bougainvillaea, not waiting for the lift or pausing until she reached her own room on the third floor and sank gasping on to the bed.

For a time she sat there, her teeth chattering with nerves and fury, her breathing rapid and shallow. Never in all her life had she been so shattered by anger. The memory of the man was vividly before her still. She could see the hard brown face, the strangely-coloured eyes, hear the contempt in his voice as he made his beastly insinuations about Ralph. About her, too. The ultimate insult—offering her that cheque as if she were

—were—— For favours received, he had said. Her friendship with Tim had been happy, innocent, and he had tried to turn it into a degrading, mercenary affair. Tears of rage gathered in her eyes and she brushed them away impatiently. But at least she had managed to hit him. I hope it hurt, she thought, beating her clenched fists against the bed. If I ever meet him again—if I ever get the chance——

She got up and strode about the room in impotent fury. It was all the worse because there was nothing she could do about what had just happened. She couldn't talk about it to Tim. After all, this man was his brother; she couldn't make trouble between them.

Gradually the rage drained away, leaving her limbs feeling like stretched elastic. She went over to the wash-basin and swilled her hands and face and drank some iced water. She wasn't going to let a man like Jason Knight get under her skin, she resolved. What he had said wasn't going to make the slightest difference to her friendship with Tim.

What had the beastly man said to Tim about her? What stories had he made up? But she had a feeling that Tim wouldn't let himself be pushed around, even by his bully of an elder brother. Tomorrow, when the Jason man had left, she would be specially nice to Tim. Not leading him on to expect anything she couldn't promise, of course, but in some small way making up to him for having such a horrid brother.

And she would be specially nice to Ralph, too. Ralph was a dear and he had been wonderfully generous to her, and she wasn't going to have a man like Jason Knight making beastly insinuations about him. She hadn't really understood what he was getting at, but whatever it was, it was untrue. Libellous, probably, she told herself, her anger flaring again. She wouldn't give the

matter another thought and she certainly wouldn't tell
Ralph about it. Instead, she would wear his favourite
dress for dinner; she would even try to like his friend
Carlos Sorano, if that was what he wanted.

Meanwhile she would stay here in her room until it
was time to dress for dinner. In no circumstances would
she risk meeting Tim's brother again today.

She pulled on a light wrap, for the room was air-
conditioned and cool, lay down on the bed and opened a
book, determining to put Jason Knight entirely out of
her mind.

She wasn't completely successful.

An hour later Sara was sitting before the mirror, putting
the finishing touches to her make-up for the evening,
when there was a tap on the door and Ralph walked in.

She turned from the dressing table with a welcoming
smile. 'Hullo, I thought you were playing cards.'

He sauntered across the room and leaned against the
window-frame, regarding her appreciatively. 'I like that
eye-shadow. New, isn't it?'

'Um!' She smoothed it delicately with her finger-tip.
She had searched her make-up box for something she
thought would please him and had finally chosen this
one called 'tropic night', a deep blue-purple with a faint
glitter, as of stars. She felt it made her look too sophisticated, but she guessed that Ralph would approve. He
liked her to look 'high fashion', as he put it.

'We'd just started a game and then Carlos had a message from his home and we had to break it up.' Ralph
looked down from the window, which overlooked the
hotel's front courtyard. 'You nearly ready?'

'Ready? Dinner won't be for an hour or more yet.' She
glanced at her tiny gold wrist-watch and added teasingly,
'You're looking very fetching this evening, Mr Francis.'

And indeed Ralph was looking at his most handsome, his fairish hair waving back immaculately from a broad forehead. She always thought that his wide face and blunt features and the deep cleft in his chin gave him a faintly theatrical look; he might have passed as a famous actor. 'But why the cover-up?' she added.

In Acapulco, evening wear for men consisted of lightweight slacks with a sheer, long-sleeved dressy shirt—pleated, tucked, embroidered, printed. The watchword was 'anything goes', and only head waiters, and newcomers who hadn't learned the ropes, wore conventional evening dress. But this afternoon Ralph was wearing a formal dark jacket and silk tie.

'Change of plans, my pretty. Carlos has been recalled to his home in Mexico.'

'Oh.' She turned back to the mirror to hide the relief that must surely show in her face. 'But I thought we were in Mexico already.'

He laughed. Ralph had a fascinating chuckle, full-throated and infectious. 'Mexico, to the natives, means Mexico City. The rest of it is *la república*, my sweet. You'd better get used to that.'

'Why should I?' she said idly, picking up her lipstick. 'We'll be moving on somewhere else soon, I expect.'

He didn't answer that, but looked down towards the forecourt again. He said, 'Can you be dressed and ready in about a quarter of an hour? We've got a car coming for us.'

'A car?'

'That's right, my dear. I've got a surprise for you. Carlos has invited us to his home for dinner and to spend the night.'

'To his home? But I thought you said he lived in Mexico City—I mean, in Mexico. Isn't it more than two hundred miles—it would take hours and hours——'

'About forty minutes, I'd say, in Carlos's private plane.' He looked as smug as if he were spreading a magic carpet before her, and she could see he was delighted with the invitation from this rich and no doubt very important man.

Sara's first reaction was to say she wouldn't go. She still felt shaky and upset after the confrontation with Tim's brother down by the pool, and the thought of spending the evening and staying the night at the house of middle-aged people was daunting. She would much prefer to have dinner sent up to her room and go to bed early, saying she had a headache. Then, in the morning, when she judged that the Jason individual had taken himself off the premises, she could go down to the pool and meet Tim and——

To gain time she asked, 'Who else will be there? Has Mr Sorano got a wife?'

'He's a widower, he tells me. Lost his wife a year ago, poor fellow.' Ralph shook his head regretfully. Then he brightened up. 'This is going to be quite something, Sara —to see the inside of a real millionaire's home.'

'When are we coming back?' she asked. She must see Tim again before he left, two days hence. She couldn't just go off without a word.

'Oh, tomorrow, I expect.' Ralph shrugged it off. 'If Carlos isn't returning we could come by the shuttle service. What will you wear, Sara? I think that caftan I bought you in Nassau would fill the bill. You look very eye-catching in that and you haven't worn it since we came here, have you? And put on plenty of jewellery. I imagine Carlos's home will be much more formal than we are here in Acapulco. Hence *my* adornment!' He fingered his tie with a grin. 'Now don't be long, there's a good girl. Just put what you'll need for the night into a case and come down as soon as you're ready. We'll be waiting in the foyer for you. Right?' He walked briskly to the door.

She watched him go and after a moment or two went after him. 'Do I——' she began, but when she reached the door the lift was already descending.

She pursed her lips and went back into the room. She had been going to say, 'Do I dress for dinner now, or put on something to travel in?' She usually asked Ralph's advice about these things; even after all these months of travelling round to smart resorts she knew that she hadn't yet quite acquired the confidence and poise to carry off all situations as she would wish. Just look at the way she had reacted to that hateful Jason Knight! She was sure, now, that she ought to have made a better job of demolishing him completely, and as she went back to the mirror and picked up a lip-brush she rehearsed all the biting things she might have said to him—and now never would.

She gathered her toilet things into their case and slid back the door of the wardrobe. The beautiful silky clothes swished under her fingers as the hangers clicked along the rail. She had a lot of lovely things; Ralph had been very generous to her in the matter of adornment.

'What's the good of having a beautiful young woman for a daughter if you don't show her off?' he had demanded with his lopsided smile, when she had at first demurred at the amount of money he was spending on her.

He had, from the beginning, chosen her clothes himself at the various boutiques they had visited on their travels. Once or twice the vendeuse had questioned his choice. 'Does Monsieur not think something a little younger, perhaps, more delicate, for Mademoiselle?' But he had always had his way in the end, and it had pleased Sara that he was proud of her and like to show her off to the acquaintances he made in the hotels they visited.

And after wearing school uniform all these years it was a thrill to own so many chic, vivid clothes. Jewelry, too. Not real stones, of course, but gorgeous chunky costume pieces—necklaces and brooches and bracelets.

She found the caftan Ralph wanted her to wear and slid into it, the clinging pure silk moulding itself to her body and swirling out when she moved. It was an exotic garment in deep vibrant, jungle colours with a provocatively slit neckline. The gold Creole earrings and matching bracelets would look right, she thought, searching in her jewel case for them. When she was ready she turned slowly before the long mirror, checking that everything was just right, that Ralph would be pleased with her. And all of a sudden, looking at the reflection of this soignée young woman who looked back at her; the elegant, sophisticated clothes; the smooth classic arrangement of her hair; the pencil-slim high-heels of the Spanish kid shoes; the huge swinging earrings; everything that went to make up the picture of the beautiful stepdaughter that Ralph Francis had fashioned out of a seventeen-year-old schoolgirl—all of a sudden, and for the very first time, Sara had a quick and painful yearning to throw it all off, to get into a cotton beachdress and run down to the pool hand-in-hand with Tim, laughing and fooling around together.

But it was ungrateful of her to moan. This invitation was evidently something that meant a great deal to Ralph, and she could, of course, back him up. Anyway, there would be plenty of time to see Tim when they returned tomorrow.

Hastily she packed her slim air-travel bag with everything she would need for the night, together with a bright pink cotton sunner to wear on the return flight. Then, with a final critical glance at the dramatic, shimmering reflection of herself in the long mirror, she went out to the lift.

The hotel foyer served as a casual meeting place and was, as usual, fairly full at this time in the early evening. People sat about in basket chairs, talking, laughing, sipping their drinks. Sara saw Ralph immediately, standing beside the bulky figure of Carlos Sorano in front of one of the glass showcases near the entrance, and she threaded her way between the tables and the pillars, lush with trailing green plants, towards them. The eyes of every man lifted as she passed, but of this she was quite unconscious.

But she caught Ralph's smile of approval as she reached him, and there was no avoiding the look of fulsome satisfaction in Carlos Sorano's plump face as he lifted her hand and pressed his moist lips against it. 'So beautiful!' he murmured in his excellent English. 'I am most honoured. Shall we go?'

He placed a hand at her elbow and led her towards the entrance, with Ralph on his other side. Sara fixed a slightly glassy smile on her mouth and allowed herself to be gently urged towards a car standing in the forecourt. They had nearly reached it when she saw Tim approaching from the direction of the path that led to the lower terraces of the hotel. Behind him was his brother Jason, and Tim was addressing some remark to him over his shoulder. Then Tim turned his head and saw her immediately.

He took a few eager steps towards her. 'Sara, there you are—I've been wondering———' He stopped, flushing as he grasped the situation.

There was nothing she could do, no explanations she could make. All that was possible was to smile at Tim and hope that somehow he would know that it was not by her own choice that she was being ushered into a large car so attentively by this man who was old enough to be her grandfather.

Tim stood quite still, staring, his usual good manners completely forgotten, as she went by with the stout Mexican holding her arm and leaning towards her possessively. Just for a split second she paused. It was only a brief flash, but in that flash she saw the whole scene as if it were frozen into a colour snapshot. Carlos Sorano and herself—Ralph on her other side, turned away to speak to an acquaintance—Tim rooted to the spot looking so young and vulnerable in dark trousers and white embroidered shirt. And behind him, his brother Jason, in some odd way seeming to dominate the whole picture. He hadn't yet changed and in the canvas shorts and limp blue cotton shirt, hanging open, his dark hair tousled as if he had been running his fingers through it, he looked a ruffian. He also looked as if he could take on any man within sight and they couldn't stand a chance against him.

He, too, was staring at Sara, but there was no dismay in *his* face, as in Tim's. No surprise, either. He looked insufferably sardonic—a man who has made his point and been proved right.

The pause was over almost before it began, but in that instant Sara met the oddly coloured eyes of Jason Knight and felt their impact like a shock passing through her whole body and gasped as if he had struck her.

The frozen instant dissolved, Jason Knight slipped his arm through his brother's and they walked on as if they had never stopped and the chauffeur was opening the door of the big car while Carlos Sorano settled Sara inside solicitously and took the seat beside her. Ralph got in and sat down opposite on the tip-up seat, and they drove away in the direction of the airport.

'You are quite comfortable, my dear Sara?' Carlos's soft voice came from beside her.

Her head jerked round. 'What—oh yes, thank you, quite comfortable,' said Sara.

But she knew she wasn't going to feel completely comfortable again until she was sure that Jason Knight had left and she was never going to see those strange, disturbing eyes of his again.


## CHAPTER TWO

CARLOS SORANO'S house, high up in wooded hills above Mexico City, was, Sara decided, like a fairy palace, complete with ogre. No, that was unfair; Carlos was no ogre, he was merely a large, fat, elderly, self-made man (he had confessed to that with some satisfaction during the plane flip from Acapulco—the self-made bit, at least!).

She had heard how friendly Mexicans were, but Carlos was a little too friendly, she felt. As he sat between herself and her stepfather in the enormous, chauffeur-driven car that had met their private plane, he seemed always to be leaning in her direction to point out places of interest as they passed them. 'The Zocala—the Cathedral—the Zona Rosa——' Here he laid a plump hand adorned with rings upon her silk-covered knee as he purred '—the fashionable quarter where you lovely ladies buy your beautiful clothes.'

He didn't remove his hand and Sara sat there, acutely embarrassed, and stared out of the window while shops, restaurants, giant skyscrapers, gardens, ancient buildings, flashed past along streets crowded with a living kaleidoscope of moving pedestrians and glossy cars, and hazy with the smoke and fumes of an enormous city that seemed not to have acquired a clean-air policy yet.

'And this,' Carlos announced as they drove along a wide avenue into a vast area of woodland, 'is our famous Chapultepec Park, undoubtedly the largest and most wonderful park in the world. Here we have everything— museums, galleries, theatres, playgrounds, boating lakes, a zoo, performing dolphins, miniature railroads——'

Sara's head swam. According to this man everything in Mexico was bigger and better than anything of its kind in the universe. And he spoke as if he owned the lot!

His house, up among the trees above the city, was even more overwhelming. Sara thought it resembled an ornately iced cake, gleaming white in the midst of a lush, semi-tropical garden. She heard Ralph's quick intake of breath as they were ushered inside, and saw his eyes shining. Her own eyes felt glassy by now and she had run out of adjectives, so she left the appreciation to him and merely followed their host as he showed off his fabulous domain. She guessed that probably some busi-ness deal that Ralph hadn't told her about hung upon the success of this visit. The insulting jibe that Jason Knight had made about her stepfather 'having bigger game in his sights' must have referred to Ralph's associa-tion with the millionaire tycoon, and when she remem-bered the contempt on the dark, hard face as he spoke, she resolved to be as pleasant as she could to Carlos Sorano, for Ralph's sake, and as if—in some obscure way —she were getting her own back on that detestable man Jason Knight.

There seemed to be no women about the house and Sara was escorted upstairs by Carlos himself, carrying her travel satchel. He opened the door of an ornate bedroom with an enormous square bed, low and satin-quilted in peach colour. 'I will leave you to rest now, *señorita*. Please ring if you desire anything more than the drinks I shall have sent up to you presently. Dinner will be at eight o'clock and until then I shall have things to talk over with your stepfather, so perhaps you will excuse us?'

'Yes, of course,' Sara told him, relieved that she was to be left alone for a while.

He hovered for a moment just inside the door. He really was much too fat for this climate, Sara thought. Beads of perspiration stood out all over his swarthy face and he took out a large white handkerchief and mopped them away.

And still he didn't go. 'You will be comfortable here, Señorita Sara?'

'Oh yes, I'm sure I shall.' Wrapped in luxury was more like it, she thought, glancing round the room, all peach and ivory, all softness and ease.

'That is good.' The purring voice was morose now. 'It was my wife's room. She was very beautiful.' His eyes, dark and mournful behind their steel-rimmed glasses, turned to a photograph on a polished wood chest—a photograph in an elaborately-tooled silver frame of a woman with a fair skin and golden hair. Carlos sighed deeply. 'But life goes on and one must find fresh comforts. A man becomes lonely.'

'Yes, of course,' Sara murmured, feeling vaguely uncomfortable.

He sighed again, and, with a long, softly smiling look at her, went out and closed the door.

Sara stood in the middle of the room, a little frown between her eyes. She supposed she should feel sorry for the man, living apparently all alone in this great showy mansion of a house, but there was something about him that repelled her. She would be very glad when this visit was over.

Dinner was served in a spacious room linked to the garden by vast glass doors, so that it was difficult to see at first where the room ended and the garden began. Feathery green plants rose from silver urns and cascaded in green loops against the white walls; bronze sculptures stood on marble-topped tables; modern pictures—great splashes of vivid colour—hung all down one long wall; ornately carved furniture, probably priceless, was displayed like a collection of showpieces not designed to be used, while in contrast, at one end of the room was a place for lounging, with deep, silver-grey sofas and chairs, low glass-topped tables on heavy beaten-silver legs.

They dined beside the open doors to the garden, with fountains plashing and white-coated, dark-skinned stewards hovering. Just four sat down to dinner. Sara had hoped that there would be a large dinner party, so that she could comfortably merge into the background, which she usually managed to do when she was included in invitations from Ralph's acquaintances.

But this time there was no escape. Quite the reverse, in fact, for it almost seemed that Carlos Sorano was making her the guest of honour. The fourth person at the table was a small man with a dark peak of hair and skin like brown leather, whom Carlos introduced as his personal secretary, José Gómez. He and her stepfather seemed to be engaged in conversation most of the time on one side of the great polished table, while Carlos sat at the head with Sara on his right. The food was unfamiliar and exotic and most of the time she hadn't the faintest idea what she was eating, though she guessed that it must be super of its kind.

'For myself,' Carlos Sorano leaned towards her and spoke in his soft, intimate voice, 'I prefer our true Mexican dishes, but for you, Señorita Sara, I felt that the heat of the chillis might blister your pretty lips, so I tell my chef to—to cool it, as they say.' He slid a playful look towards her and she smiled back politely.

When dinner was over Carlos ushered Sara to one of the deep sofas and turned to select a liqueur for her to drink with her coffee. He poured a dark liquid into a crystal glass and handed it to her with a beaming smile.

'I—I really think I've had enough to drink,' she told him. She had had far more wine at dinner than usual and was beginning to feel very warm and rather dizzy.

'Just a leetle sip, *señorita*,' Carlos urged. 'It is *muy bueno*—vairy good.' He sat himself down on the sofa, close beside her, and Ralph took a big chair opposite.

Sara drank her coffee and out of politeness managed a little of the fiery liqueur before she put the glass down with a little gasp, as her throat was burning.

Their host turned to her solicitously. 'You are not feeling unwell, I trust, *señorita*?'

She touched her hot cheeks. 'No, thank you. Just a little warm.'

'Ah yes—our terrible climate! We will go out into the garden, it will be more cool there, and I can show you some of my treasures.'

He stood up and Sara followed suit. It would be a relief to get into the open air. She looked across to where her stepfather was lying back in the deep chair opposite, puffing appreciatively at a huge cigar. The secretary had excused himself after dinner and disappeared to another part of the house.

'You'd like to see the garden too, Ralph?' Sara willed him to come.

'Ah, but I'm so very comfortable where I am. *And*

lazy!' He grinned up at her through the cigar smoke. 'Do
excuse me, Carlos, and take Sara out. I'll see your lovely
garden another time.'

A glance passed between to two men and Carlos said,
'But certainly, *mi amigo*, make yourself comfortable.' He
held out an arm to Sara. 'Shall we go, *señorita*?'

Sara gave Ralph a pleading look, but he was leaning
back with his eyes closed, the picture of contentment.
There was nothing for it but to go with the fat tycoon.
Trying not to show her reluctance, she put her fingers on
his arm, and he grasped her hand and tucked it into the
crook of his elbow, holding it fast against him as he led
her out into the garden.

It was certainly cooler outside, but still a very warm
night. There was no moon and in the starlight the garden
was a mass of dark shapes criss-crossed by the lighter
stone of the pathways. As they walked along paved ave-
nues between the shadowy flowerbeds the secent was almost overpowering.

'You feel better in the air, yes?' Carlos leaned solicitously towards Sara.

'Yes, thank you,' she murmered politely, wondering if
she could suggest returning to the house without seeming rude.

'That is good. I will show you something very special,
now.' He pressed her arm more firmly against him and
she could feel the damp heat of his body through the
light jacket he wore.

At the end of another long path, and under an arch,
they were in a small clearing surrounded by the shapes of
high bushes. In the starlight Sara could just make out a
strange, dim building that stood in the centre of the
clearing. It loomed above them, grey and mysterious, its
domed top showing vague colours against the sky.

'This,' purred Carlos Sorano proudly,' is my own small

temple. It was made to my order, so that I should feel happy in my house here. My home, you see, was in Mérida and I consider myself Yucateco first and Mexicano second. Inside one of the great pyramids, where I was taken as a child, is a secret temple containing a jaguar with eyes inlaid with jade. It made a great impression on me. This is not a copy of the temple, you understand—just a reminder. In your country you would call it a folly.'

He leaned down and touched something at the base of the building and immediately the whole clearing was flooded with stark white light. In the doorway of the building stood a horrific animal with wide-open jaws and long fangs and great staring glassy green eyes.

'My leetle Jaguar—he is very beautiful, do you not think so?' Carlos stroked the animal head lovingly. 'My ancestors once worshipped the Jaguar god.'

Sara shivered. 'He terrifies me.'

'Ah, no, he is quite tame, he would not hurt anybody. We are not cruel now as once was perhaps the case. In ancient days there was a sacred well in the real temple. They would adorn their beautiful maidens with jewels and throw them into the well, as sacrifices to Chac, the god of rain.' His hot, pudgy hand stroked her arm. 'We do not sacrifice our maidens any longer,' he chuckled. 'We have better things to do with them. I make a leetle joke, yes?'

To her horror he pulled the silk of her caftan from her shoulder and placed his mouth against her flesh.

'No!' She drew away sharply, feeling faintly sick.

He chuckled again. 'You are shy, señorita. I like that. I like that very much. Now we will rejoin your stepfather, yes?'

'Yes, please,' said Sara in a muffled voice. 'I think I'm feeling a little unwell. I should like to go to bed soon.

If that doesn't seem rude,' she added, remembering why she was here—to help Ralph's business ventures. There was, she admitted to herself, nothing very terrible about what the fat elderly Mexican had done; in fact, she thought he was rather pathetic. It was just that she couldn't bear to touch him or have him near her.

'Of course,' he said immediately. 'I am so very sorry. If there is anything I can do—a doctor, perhaps? I have a friend who——'

'No—please,' she said hastily. 'It's just the heat, I'm sure. I shall be perfectly all right in the morning.' She quickened her steps towards the house until she was almost running.

Ralph was still sitting at ease, smoking his cigar. Sara stood before him, holding the silky caftan closely round her. 'I'm not feeling too good,' she said. 'I'm going up to bed.'

Her stepfather was on his feet immediately, frowning, looking from her to Carlos, who had come in behind her, panting slightly.

'Señorita Sara is feeling the strain of the altitude; it is very common, you know, for visitors. We are very high, up here. I think it better that she should rest.'

The frown disappeared from Ralph's forehead. 'Yes, yes, of course.' He sounded relieved now, concerned. 'I'm sorry, my dear, is there anything I can get for you?'

'Nothing, thanks.' She just wanted to get away as quickly as possible. 'I know my way—I'll go up now. Goodnight, both of you.' She smiled fleetingly in the direction of the two men and fled up the wide marble staircase to the sanctuary of her bedroom, where she slipped out of the caftan and lay down on the bed, breathing quickly.

It was some time before she calmed down. It was stupid, really, this feeling of being threatened, she told herself. Nothing had happened, nothing. She didn't think she had offended the too-friendly Señor Sorano, or let Ralph down, but she would be thankful to get away in the morning. Once back in Acapulco she wouldn't have to meet the fat tycoon again, thank goodness.

Getting away proved easier than she had expected. The following morning Ralph informed her that Carlos had been called away to a business meeting in Texas, and had already left, sending his apologies. After lunch a car would drive them to the airport, where they would take a plane on the shuttle service back to Acapulco.

Sara breathed a sigh of relief when she received this information. 'Oh, good!'

Ralph gave her a quick look, but said nothing. In fact, he was unusually quiet on the return journey, and it wasn't until he had carried Sara's bag up to her room in the hotel that the blow fell that would alter Sara's whole life.

Her stepfather settled himself in a basket chair by the window and lit a cigarette. He had the air of a man well satisfied with life. 'Well, the visit was definitely a success, don't you think? What a man! He must be a millionaire several times over. Fabulous place he has there!'

He blew out smoke and looked up at the ceiling and then back at Sara, perched on the edge of the bed. But she didn't respond. She was wondering where Tim was and how soon she could contact him. After her experience with Carlos Sorano she felt she needed Tim's straightforward, breezy company to make her feel young and happy again. As soon as she could get rid of Ralph, she would change into her sun-suit and go down and look for Tim. That beastly brother of his should have left by now.

Ralph was still talking on. '—had a long chat together

last night after you'd gone to bed. He's one of the keen men who made a packet when Mexico began to move into the top league, some years ago. His firm makes gear and machinery for the oil fields, you know.'

Sara brought her thoughts back and tried to show an interest. 'But you're not concerned with machinery, surely?'

'Me? Good lord, no. Why?'

'I—I thought you were perhaps doing some sort of business with Mr Sorano, and that's why he invited us to his home.'

There was a silence. Ralph crossed his legs, looking down at his feet in their hand-made shoes of soft, pale leather. Then he looked up at her and said confidentially, 'I'll tell you something, Sara. When I saw you at that boarding school of yours, I thought, This girl is a beauty, but more than that, I saw you had spirit, that you'd be fun to take along with me on my travels. I knew we'd see things the same way, get along together. And we have, haven't we?'

'Ye-es,' she said, and then more firmly, 'Yes, of course we have.'

'I thought, There's a girl who'd stick by a bloke, wouldn't let him down. Would want to repay what he spent on her, if he fell on hard times. And I know now that my first guess was right. I know how sweet you are—how kind and loyal.'

'But——' She looked round the expensive, luxurious bedroom in bewilderment. 'But you haven't fallen on hard times, have you?'

He grinned his rueful, lopsided grin. 'You brought me luck at first, Sara, but it's turned sour on me. You can't win 'em all, as they say. The fact is'—he ground out his cigarette, taking his time over it—'the fact is, I'm broke, Sara love, broke to the wide. I'm in your hands, my sweet.' He spread out his own hands in an eloquent gesture of supplication. 'I'm asking for your help.'

'But of course,' she said immediately. 'I'll work—there must be something I could do. Hotel work or something. We'll get together and think it out. Perhaps we could get back to England and I could train for something, or——'

The eager words faltered away at the look on his face. 'Work? You don't think I was talking about work, do you?'

'Then what—what can I do?'

His smile was tolerant. 'Don't you know why Carlos invited us to his house? Don't tell me you're as green as that.'

'Green? What do you mean—green?'

'My dear child! Well, if I have to spell it out for you —the reason was you.'

'Me?' she echoed again, stupidly. A cold knot of fear was forming inside her somewhere.

'Yes, you!' He waited for a moment for that to sink in. 'Carlos wants to marry you, my dear, how about that for hitting the jackpot?'

She stared, her throat dry. Finally she croaked, 'Marry me? Oh, goodness, how awful! Whatever am I going to say to him?'

He looked amused. 'What any sensible girl would say, I should think. "Yes sir, please sir." '

'You're not—you're not serious?' He must be joking, he *must*; in another minute they would be laughing together as they often did, seeing the funny side of this. Because it *was* funny, she thought wildly. It was the funniest thing that had happened since they had been together. Marry Carlos Sorano! She tried to laugh, but her mouth was stiff and the cold knot of fear inside her was spreading all over her body. She stared at Ralph, lounging there in his chair, and she saw something in his face that she had never seen before. He looked— calculating. And cold.

'I'm dead serious. I've never beèn more serious in my life,' he said.

Her lips began to tremble. 'But I couldn't—it's impossible. It's——' She fumbled in her mind for a word that would convey the utter impossibility of what he was suggesting. 'It's—obscene!'

He produced his lopsided smile. 'Oh come, my dear, it's not as bad as that, surely? Carlos is what I believe they used to call a fine figure of a man.'

She shuddered. 'He's—fat—and horrid—and I can't bear him near me. And—and he's *old*!' She stood up, but her knees felt so weak that she sat down again quickly.

'He's sixty-two, he tells me. Not really old.'

'And I'm eighteen. You *can't* mean it, you can't. You can't make me marry him. You can't make me marry anyone. We're not living in—in the Middle Ages!' Her voice rose thinly. She should be talking to him reasonably, a small voice inside her said, showing him how ridiculous his suggestion was and why he couldn't expect her to fall in with it, but the shock had left her mind spinning like a top and she was afraid she was going to burst into tears. Even now she could feel them welling up at the back of her eyes.

Ralph got up and walked over to the bed, putting a hand on her silky pale hair. 'Of course I can't make you,' he said smoothly. 'All I can do is point out the advantages. Or shall we say the immediate *disadvantages*, the most important of which is that I'm skint and the hotel won't give me any more credit—unless, that is, I can tell them that my stepdaughter is the fiancée of Señor Sorano. Then the sky would be the limit.' He sat down beside her on the bed. 'So you see, my dear,' he said softly, 'I'm afraid I should have to leave you to fend for yourself. Personally, I should go to ground, as has become unfortunately necessary before now.'

Sara listened with a growing horror as the whimsical voice went on, just as if she were a child and he were persuading her to forget her shyness and go to a party.

'I shouldn't be able to take you along with me, I'm afraid. Of course I suppose you might get a job of some kind, although it would be difficult as you don't speak the language. And of course you haven't any training for anything, have you? I shouldn't be able to leave you with any cash, naturally, because I haven't got any myself. So don't you think it might turn out a little difficult for you? If you do decide to go it alone, I ought to warn you that Mexico is still a man's country and the men are extremely—er—*macho*. In case you don't know the word, it means virile—sexually competent, if you see what I mean, so you'd have to watch your step.'

Helpless tears were running down Sara's cheeks now and she couldn't speak.

Ralph stood up. 'Well now, I'll leave you to think it over. I can see it's been a bit of a surprise to you, but I'm sure when you've had time to consider you'll admit that there really isn't much choice. Be a sensible girl now, and put on your prettiest dress and be ready to greet Carlos with a smile when he arrives. He's flying back here and will join us for dinner.' He walked to the door. 'I'll come back in an hour or so, when you've had time to make up your mind.' His hand on the doorknob, he chuckled, as she had so often heard him chuckle when something amused him. 'You'll make a very beautiful and very rich young widow,' he said, and went out of the room.

Sara sat staring at the closed door, gripped by a feeling of panic that was turning her blood to water inside her.

She must get away—she must get out of here. She pulled herself up and stumbled to the door. It was locked. She pulled at it, rattled it helplessly. She went across to the window and looked down at the scene below. Her room overlooked the garages and there were one or two people moving around between the parked cars. It was too far away to call down without yelling and that might start some sort of emergency, and make things worse than they were.

She was icy cold now and her teeth were chattering. How could she have been so blind all these months as not to see what Ralph really was? Just a con-man. But she knew she couldn't possibly have guessed. He was an expert; he lived by his charm, it was his stock-in-trade, and it must have been the easiest thing in the world for him to take in a girl of seventeen. Just now, though, she had seen for the first time what lay beneath that charm : a callousness that froze her, and terrified her. He was desperate, he'd do anything to make her do what he wanted, use any threat.

She *had* to get away, how or where to she didn't know, but anything was better than sitting here until he came back. Stifling a sob, she turned to the telephone—she'd try to explain to the receptionist somehow that she was locked in. She just had to hope that whoever was there would understand English—some of the staff did, but not all.

There was a sick feeling in her stomach as she put out her hand to the receiver. And then the instrument began to buzz.

She snatched the receiver off. 'Yes?'

'Sara! Hullo, Sara darling,' said Tim's voice. 'I saw you come back with your stepfather and I've been waiting about for you to come out. Are you coming for a swim?'

'Tim, I——' The sudden relief of hearing his voice was too much for her. 'I——' she tried again chokily, and stopped.

'Sara—Sara darling, what's up? You're crying.'

Somehow she got control of herself. 'Tim—listen, and don't ask anything yet. I'm locked in and I can't get out. Could you get another key, do you think? I must—I *must* get out,' she finished desperately.

There was the shortest of pauses. Then Tim's voice said, 'Hang on, I'll be with you,' and the line went dead.

She stood beside the door, hardly breathing. If Ralph should come back—if he should encounter Tim—it would be cruel to involve Tim in a degrading scene—when she heard the whine of the lift and the grating of the key in the lock a few minutes later she felt as if she were going to faint.

But it was Tim who opened the door. He took one look at her and his face changed. Pushing the door closed with his foot, he put an arm round her and led her to the bed, sitting down beside her.

'Now,' he said gently, 'tell me.'

She shook her head, biting her lip hard. 'It's wrong to bring you into this. Now the door's unlocked I can——'

She half rose, but he pulled her back firmly. 'Tell me,' he said again. 'You may as well tell me what's happened, because we're going to sit here until you do.' His arm tightened round her.

Hesitantly she looked up at him and saw a strength in his fair, pleasant face that she hadn't seen before. Tim wasn't a boy any longer.

'It's Ralph—my stepfather,' she said in a low voice. 'I —I've suddenly found out what he's like. He's going to make me marry Carlos Sorano.'

'Sorano? That fat slob?' Tim's voice rose in horror.

'Ssh!' She put a hand warningly on his arm and looked around as if there were someone listening in the room.

'But he can't!' Tim lowered his voice. 'It's absolutely ludicrous and disgusting. Don't worry, Sara love, nobody can make you marry if you don't want to. You must have misunderstood him.' He gave her a reassuring squeeze. 'Don't panic, Sara, you're over age; your stepfather hasn't got any power over you.'

'I think he has,' she said very slowly. 'And he knows it.'

She saw now that Tim was her only lifeline and now that she had told him so much she must tell him the rest, and ask for his help. So, word for word, she told him what Ralph had just said to her and she could feel his arm tighten protectively round her as she went on.

When she had finished he drew in a long breath. 'The bastard!' he muttered. 'The dirty—well, never mind. Didn't you guess what sort of man he was?'

She shook her head helplessly. 'I've only known him a few months. He came to the school and took me away to give me a home. He was kind and charming, and bought me nice clothes and took me to exciting places. And all the time he was looking on me as a kind of—of insurance policy. He said I was green, and how right he was!' She straightened her back. 'But this isn't your problem, Tim dear. If you could just lend me enough money to get away somewhere. I could go back to Mexico City perhaps—it's so huge he'd never find me there and bring me back to put pressure on me. And once I'd got away from him I could—I could——'

Tim was regarding her tenderly. 'Yes, my poor silly darling, what could you do then?'

'I'd think of something. I'd go to the British Consul, or Ambassador, or whatever they have and ask him——'

'And don't you think that's the first place that step-

father of yours would look for you?' Tim asked with a
grim smile. 'And can't you imagine the tale he would
tell? Hysterical young daughter, unfortunate love affair
—these young girls! You'd find yourself back where you
started. Your stepfather's got a lot at stake—he won't
give up that easily.'

'Well then, I——'

Tim put a large hand over her mouth very gently.
'Now you shush, my darling girl, and I'll tell you what's
going to happen. I'm sorry you're upset about all this,
but I can't be sorry that it's put all the aces in the pack
into my hands. Because now I'm going to look after you.
First of all I'm going to get you away from that un-
speakable man. Have you got your papers? Passport?
Tourist card?'

She nodded. 'Yes, they're there in my bag. Ralph
always said I'd better have them in case we got—
separated.' She grimaced. 'I expect he must have always
been considering the possibility of going off alone and
ditching me if things went wrong for him.'

He muttered something inaudible, then he stood up
and pulled her to her feet. 'Bring your handbag, then.
Can you stuff a nightie and a toothbrush in it? That's all
you'd better take. If you were seen with a suitcase someone might begin asking questions.'

Her white handbag was fairly capacious. She checked,
with fumbling fingers, that her papers were in it; then she
found a nightie, a change of pants and bra and a toothbrush, pushed them in and pulled the zipper. She hesi-
tated, looking round. 'Shouldn't I leave a note or something? If he found I'd disappeared he might—he might
put the police on to find me.'

Tim thought for a moment. Then he got out his pocket
book and pencil and scribbled on a page; tore it out and
placed it in the middle of the bed.

Sara leaned down to read what he had written. In Tim's round, schoolboyish hand it said: I'm taking Sara away. It won't be worth your trouble trying to find us because she won't be any use to you now. She'll be married to me. T. Knight.

She looked up at him, standing behind her very tall and slim and resolute, and her eyes were enormous. 'But Tim, I told you I couldn't—'

'That was yesterday,' he said, 'and things have changed.' His arm went round her encouragingly. 'Come on, my love, there's no time to lose. You *are* going to marry me, aren't you?'

There were so many things she should have said, so many reasons why she should refuse, but she couldn't think of any of them.

'Aren't you?' he repeated gently.

'Oh, Tim,' she whispered, her eyes swimming. 'I'll make it up to you. I swear I will.'

It seemed an odd way to accept a proposal of marriage. She wished she could tell him she was in love with him, but she couldn't. Falling in love was something that hadn't happened to her, but when it did she hoped it would be with Tim.

He took her hand and his mouth twisted. 'To listen to you, my love, anyone would think I was doing you a favour, instead of being the luckiest chap alive!' He gazed wonderingly into the huge violet-blue eyes, still wet with tears. Then his voice changed, became brisk. 'Now come on, we've got to hurry to get out of here. You'd better park in my room while I check out and pack my things. Then I'll do a recce to make sure your stepfather is well out of the way. After that we'll make for the airport and chance our luck.'

Sara had the feeling of being carried along by a strong

tide. She gave him a small, admiring smile. 'You think of everything, Tim,' she said.

Twenty-four hours later, in a smaller and much more modest hotel room, she put the same thought into different words. 'You've been absolutely marvellous, Tim. I simply can't believe it's all happened!'

He grinned modestly. 'Luck's been on our side. Getting seats on that flight—then managing to find these rooms—then the fact that it's incredibly easy to get married in Mexico if you're a tourist. Oh gosh, Sara!' His eyes kindled as he picked up her left hand with the gleaming new wedding ring on it. 'I can't really believe it either.'

They stood hand in hand at the window of the small hotel in Mexico City looking down at the busy street below, with the park just within sight. Sara had been nervous about coming back to the city, as if Carlos Sorano might be lurking around every corner, but Tim had laughed away her fears. 'He'd have a job to find you! This big haystack has more than eight million inhabitants, so they tell me, and you're a very small needle, my sweet!'

All the same, when they left the Civil Register Office after the short, dry marriage ceremony, Sara insisted on going back to the hotel, where they had a very late lunch and then made plans—or rather, Tim made plans and Sara, with a feeling that she was beginning to wake up after a particularly horrid nightmare, agreed with everything he suggested.

'I've still got two days left of my holiday,' he told her. 'Let's make it into a honeymoon.' He glanced at her shyly, doubtfully. 'I don't mean—that is, you know how I feel, but I'm not going to hurry you or anything.'

He flushed rather painfully. 'I know you're not in love with me, but——'

'Oh, Tim!' Sara was almost in tears again, and it suddenly occurred to her that she had shed more tears in the last couple of days than in the rest of her eighteen years. 'Tim darling, of course I'm not going to hold out on you. We'll have a lovely honeymoon.'

He looked at her adoringly, as if she had handed him the moon and the stars on a plate, and then went out to make enquiries and arrangements. An hour later he was back at the hotel with the news that he had booked a sleeper on the night train to Veracruz. 'They suggested it at the travel place, and I thought it might be a good idea to see the other side of Mexico, the Gulf side. We could have a couple of days there and come back here in time to meet Jason. He's in Yucatan just now, drumming up orders.' He chuckled. 'Golly, won't we have a surprise for him?'

'Surprise?' Sara pulled a wry face. 'From what he said to me I'd have thought it was going to be a very nasty shock!' Facing Tim's brother was something she wasn't looking forward to at all, but she consoled herself with the fact that circumstances had changed considerably since that encounter by the hotel pool. For one thing, she was Tim's wife now. For another—and she had to be honest about this—he had perhaps had a certain amount of justice on his side. He must have known far more about Ralph's shady exploits than she knew herself. In fact, at that time, she had believed that Ralph was all he seemed to be, but Jason Knight had evidently known better, and he had taken it for granted that she was in league with her stepfather.

Forgivable, perhaps. But when all excuses had been made for him she still couldn't forget the way he had tackled her, the arrogant, high-handed self-importance of the man. There was something hard and inflexible about him that she found frightening. She hoped she was wrong, and that his personality would mellow when she knew him better, but her eyes were anxious as she met Tim's, adding, 'I'm afraid your brother hasn't got a very good first impression of me.'

Tim stuck out his chin. 'Then he'll have to alter it pretty sharpish, and I shall tell him so in no uncertain terms.' He frowned. 'But I didn't know he'd spoken to you—I didn't know you two knew each other. What did he say?' He looked so worried that she guessed that the two brothers must have had a clash over her already.

There was no point in making things worse. 'Oh, nothing much. I just got the feeling that he didn't altogether approve of your friendship with me, that's all. But perhaps I was mistaken.'

Tim's hands clenched. 'He'd no right to speak to you about it. Jason's getting altogether too bossy. He thinks he can run my life for me, but he's got to find out that I'm my own man—and a married man, too, which is more than he can say for himself.'

'He isn't married?' she asked idly.

'No, not on your life! Jason's too fond of his own freedom. And of course he has all the girls swooning over him, he can take his pick.' He slanted a grin at her. 'And if that sounds like sour grapes, perhaps——'

'Perhaps what?' Her eyes teased him.

'Perhaps it is. Being a younger brother isn't the happiest of positions, especially when both one's parents died a long time ago and you've sort of come to look on Big Brother as the boss who gives the orders.' He squared his shoulders. 'But no longer. Timothy Knight will in future take his rightful place as partner in the firm of Knight and Sons, Boatbuilders, Dorset, England. I'll have to take you back home at first, my sweet, and

introduce you to Aunt Vera, who looks after the running
of the house for us and is rather a pet. But then we'll find
a small place just for ourselves—a cottage by the sea. It'll
be heaven to spend the rest of our lives together.'

For a long time afterwards she was to remember how
he had looked at her when he said that, how his face had
lit up, how happy he had been.

'It sounds lovely,' said Sara, and indeed it did. Just
now she would trade all the baking jet-set playgrounds in
the sun for the open heaths of Dorset, with the wind in
her hair and the soft rain on her cheeks.

They had been sitting in Sara's hotel room and now
Tim stood up and walked purposefully across to the telephone on the table beside the bed. 'I don't particularly
want to do this,' he said 'but maybe I'd better practise
my new role as a responsible citizen by getting in touch
with Jason, to put him in the picture.' He took a notebook from his pocket. 'He gave me the number of his
hotel in Mérida just in case I needed to contact him. If
he's not in I can leave a message.'

His smile was determined and his hand was firm as he
lifted the receiver. *Quiero poner una conferencia a
Mérida. Si. Mérida.'* Sara's eyebrows went up admiringly
as he gave the number and she went and sat beside him
on the bed, as if she needed to protect him. He grinned
at her and whispered, 'I took a crash course in the lingo
before we set out. How am I doing?'

'I'm most impressed,' she smiled at him. 'I only know
about three words myself.'

There was quite a wait, but eventually Tim straightened up. 'Hotel Mérida? *Quiero hablar con el Señor
Knight, por favor? Si. Su hermano.'* He turned to Sara
again. 'They think he came in just now—they're sending
someone to look for him.'

They sat side by side in silence and Sara could feel

the tension in Tim's hand, grasping hers. Her own throat was tight and she found that she was holding her breath. Stupid, of course, there was no earthly reason to be scared of Tim's brother and she must get over it quickly. It was just the vestiges of the feeling she had had in his presence—the shock of his unexpected aggression and the impact of his formidable personality. The dark, strong face with the curiously magnetic clay-coloured eyes under their thick brows seemed to jump right out of her memory, and when Tim moved beside her jerkily, and she heard his voice say, 'Jason?' she felt her heart begin to thump against her ribs.

'Jason?' Tim said again. 'Yes, Tim here. How are things going with you?'

The line was poor and the voice at the other end of the line was merely a low blur, which ceased when Tim began to talk rather quickly. 'A surprise for you, old boy. Something you ought to know. Do I sound on top of the world? Wait for it—I've just got married!'

The silence at the other end of the line was almost audible.

Tim went on quickly. 'I can't possibly explain now, Jason, it'll all have to wait until we meet up here on Tuesday, as arranged. We're in Mexico City, staying at a small hotel, and we're off to Veracruz in a few minutes—catching the night train. Who? Sara, of course —Sara Tildesley. She's here beside me now, bless her. Will you have a word with her? Jason—Jason, are you still there?'

He turned to Sara with a shrug. 'The line's gone dead, we must have been cut off.' He replaced the receiver. 'Never mind, there'll be lots of time for him to give us his blessing when we meet up on Tuesday.'

'W-what did he say?' Sara asked in a small voice, and Tim shrugged.

'Nothing, really.' For a moment his face was clouded. Then he brightened again. 'Come on, love, let's find our way to the station and have plenty of time to catch the train.'

## CHAPTER THREE

'This is jolly comfy.' Tim bounced up and down cheerfully on the springy mattress as the Pullman train gathered speed after leaving Buenavista station. 'You know, Sara, I think it was a brainwave to travel by rail. That stepfather of yours might just have suspected that my note was a bluff and that we weren't married at all, and he might have started to make enquiries at the airport. But he'd never think of looking for you on a train.'

Sara sank down beside him with a sigh of relief. There was something reassuring in the steady clatter of the train wheels and in the view passing the window of Mexico City disappearing into the evening mist. 'It's marvellous that we're getting further and further away from Ralph and—and'—she bit her lip—'and everything.'

Now that she was a married woman and Ralph could no longer threaten her life, the nightmare of the past two days was slowly receding. 'Perhaps we'll even be able to laugh at all this in time. The saga of Sara and the fat Mexican! Poor old Carlos, he was just pathetic and rather revolting—but Ralph was——' She shuddered, remembering. 'It's the worst thing that can happen when someone you've loved and trusted suddenly turns into a—a monster.'

Tim drew her close. 'But you feel safe now? You trust me?'

She put her hand in his. 'Yes,' she said solemnly, 'I do trust you.'

His young face was suddenly serious and he held her hand very tightly. 'We'll make a go of it,' he promised. 'We'll show Jason——' He broke off, glancing wryly towards her. 'Look how that man's conditioned me to need his approval! I didn't mean to bring him into this. This is *our* honeymoon, and I don't care a hoot whether he approves or not, so long as you like me just a bit, Sara darling.'

'Of course I——' she began. She looked up into Tim's face, and suddenly she forgot herself, and her own feelings, and saw all that *he* was feeling, the hope, the doubt, the longing. Impulsively she reached up and put her arms round his neck. 'Oh, Tim,' she said huskily, 'you're a wonderful person and it's more than "like". I love you, Tim, I do really.'

He looked so shaken that for a moment she thought he was going to cry. But he drew in a deep breath. 'Then that's fine,' he said boyishly, and held her very tightly, his cheek pressing against hers.

But after a while he drew away. 'You look tired, my sweet, I'm not going to rush you. But we ought to celebrate. We'll have a bottle of wine with our dinner.' He clicked his tongue. 'Gosh, what an idiot I am! I clean forgot to enquire if there's a dining car on this train; there was such a crush at the station. But I expect there is. What do you feel like—just a snack, or the full treatment?'

'Definitely just a snack,' said Sara. 'I'm more thirsty than hungry.'

He stood up. 'Done! I'll go and see what they can produce.'

At the door of the compartment he turned back and

smiled at her very tenderly. 'Be here when I come back, won't you?' he said.

He pulled the door to, and disappeared along the corridor.

Sara got up and stood looking out of the window. The train was picking up speed quickly now, leaving the sprawling outskirts of Mexico City behind. She began to feel almost happy. She had been incredibly lucky, she knew, for without Tim her situation would have been desperate—all alone in a strange country with no money and not knowing the language.

She still had a faintly uneasy feeling about what she had done, whether it had been fair to Tim to marry him. She knew, with deep intuition, that she was too young to marry anyone yet, too sexually unawakened, but perhaps the old wives' tale that love comes after marriage, not before, would be true for her. Even if it didn't, even if it proved that Tim wasn't the one to rouse her to the ultimate ecstasy that every girl knows of and hopes for, she could surely make *him* happy, and that was what mattered most. If she had lied to him just now, when she told him she loved him, then she was glad she had lied, she thought fiercely.

The light had faded now and the long train was rushing forward into the darkness. She turned from the carriage window and opened her handbag to take out comb and make-up, and saw the blue plastic folder that contained her passport and other papers. Her brand new marriage certificate was there now, with the rest, and she took it out and read it again. Timothy Knight. Sara Tildesley. There it was, in a funny, foreign handwriting. It seemed to make it all more real and believable. She sighed as she replaced it in the folder.

It was very hot in the compartment; no air-conditioning in this train, evidently. She swilled her face at the washbasin, renewed her make-up, combed her silky fair hair, cleaned her teeth, but still Tim hadn't returned. She wished he would come back. Being alone made her feel jittery again.

She went to the door and looked along the corridor. He had gone towards the front of the train and she thought she would follow, to find him. The train was travelling at speed now, rocking from side to side a little, and she put out a hand to steady herself as she stepped out into the corridor.

Then, with mind-numbing suddenness, the rocking intensified, became monstrous, grotesque, as the whole coach lurched from side to side, hurling her back into the compartment, while her hands clutched frantically for support and found nothing to hold on to.

She was on the floor now, mind reeling, ears deafened by the obscene screech of metal on metal. Then, with a great tearing, rending, crashing thud it was over. In the uncanny silence and stillness that followed she heard a thin scream and didn't know it was she herself who screamed. Something enormous and heavy was coming down on her. Her eyes closed and she knew nothing more.

Time ceased to register. There were dull, drowsy wakings and slipping back into nothingness again. There were noises and voices but no words that had meaning. There were lights that came and went behind her closed eyelids. Sometimes there was a beating and throbbing in her head; sometimes it was numb and solid, as if it were not part of her body at all.

But at last she was really awake, seeing, hearing. There was a pretty, dark-coloured face smiling down at her with a white smile that had a glint of gold in it. A soft voice murmured, '*Muy bien*,' and then some more words that she didn't understand. *Bien* must mean 'good', she thought vaguely. It must be good, then, she must hang on to that. She drifted back to sleep again.

Next time she opened her eyes she was aware of everything around her. She lay in a bed in a small room with cream-coloured walls and the sun was slanting in between blue curtains. A nurse was sitting beside the bed; she remembered the pretty face, the white teeth.

Then memory surged back sickly : the train—the dark chaos—Tim. Oh God—Tim! 'My husband—is he all right?' she whispered.

''usband?' The nurse leaned towards her, forehead creased.

'Yes—husband. My *husband*——' Oh heaven, what was it in Spanish? With an effort she pointed towards her wedding ring. 'Husband?' she said.

The young nurse beamed. 'Ah *si, si*. 'usband—*su marido*.' She stood up, smiling still and pointing towards the door, saying more incomprehensible words. Here she nodded encouragingly and went out.

Sara closed her eyes, weak with relief. Tim was safe, he must be. The nurse had gone to get him.

She drifted away into sleep again and it seemed only a moment before her arm was being shaken gently. 'Señora Knight, *señora, su marido está acquía*.'

There was a different nurse beside the bed now, an older woman. Sara stared at her desperately. Why didn't they speak so that she could understand? She lifted her hands in a helpless gesture.

'Ah—*Entiendo*—I speak *inglés*, then? Your 'usband, *el* Señor Knight, he waits.' She waved a sturdy hand towards the door. 'You see him—*si?*'

'Oh yes—yes, please,' breathed Sara fervently.

The Sister—she must be a Sister—went to the door. She was a large woman but walked with amazing light-

ness. She opened the door and spoke to someone outside, and Sara could hear a man's voice replying. *Tim*,
she thought, dizzy with the relief and joy of knowing he
was safe.

The Sister was coming back across the room now;
Sara followed her progress with her eyes, because it hurt
to move her head, and could glimpse Tim's tall figure
behind her. 'Your 'usband,' smiled the Sister, and moved
aside.

'Tim,' breathed Sara. 'Oh Tim, darling, you're safe!'

The smile froze on her lips and in the silence that
followed her words she heard the click of the door as
it closed behind the Sister. With sick, terrified foreboding
Sara stared up into the hard, dark face of Jason Knight.

She tried to lick her lips, but her tongue was dry and
felt swollen. 'Tim?' she mouthed.

The strange, clay-coloured eyes were fixed on her face
and she felt dread mounting inside her, choking her.
'*Please*——' she tried to say, but nothing came.

From outside the room there was the sound of voices.
Somebody laughed. Inside, in the heavy silence, Sara's
eyes searched the hard face above her for some sign of
sympathy, of feeling, but there was none.

At last he said in a voice so bleak that it was hardly
human, 'Tim is dead. How does it feel to be responsible
for that?'

Her eyes dilated. 'No——' the word was a croak.
'No—no—no—!'

'Yes,' came the harsh, accusing voice. 'Tim is dead and
you are alive.' He swung away from the bed as if he
couldn't bear to look at her any longer. As he turned
away he muttered something. In her shocked state Sara
couldn't tell if he had spoken the words or not. She
thought he said, 'And by God, I'll make you pay.'

Perhaps she had imagined the words; perhaps the

look on his face had put them into her mind. She didn't
know, for she had sunk back into unconsciousness.

Sara lived through days so black with misery that there
was no light at the end of the tunnel. She knew vaguely
that everyone was trying to be kind—the doctors, the
nurses, everyone—but most of the time she didn't really
understand what they said and she didn't care. She
didn't care about anything and she submitted to all the
tests and examinations without interest. But they
couldn't make her eat.

After a day or two she was moved into a larger room
with five other women, who smiled and nodded at her in
a friendly way, and chattered among themselves incom-
prehensibly while Sara lay with closed eyes and wanted
to die. Perhaps if she didn't eat at all she *would* die,
just fade away quietly into nothing. That seemed a good
solution.

Then, one evening just after a nurse had clicked her
tongue as she removed the untouched plate of food, an
English voice said, 'Hullo, Sara,' and she was startled
into opening her eyes.

A tall youngish woman in a white coat was standing
beside the bed, regarding her quizzically. She had red-
dish hair and freckles and a wide, humorous mouth.
'Well now, Sara, are you going to decide to stay with
us, after all?' she enquired briskly. 'From what I hear,
it's about time.'

Something in Sara responded feebly to hearing an English voice, but she didn't want to be brought back to
life. She wanted to die. She closed her eyes again and
turned her head away.

'Come *on* now,' the voice urged. 'Nothing's ever as bad
as that.'

How dared she be cheerful—she didn't know, how
could she? For the first time Sara felt an emotion that

wasn't misery. It was anger. 'Go away, can't you, and leave me alone,' she blurted into the pillow.

'*That's* better,' the soft unruffled voice encouraged her. 'It'll do you a power of good to get into a real paddy.' There was a scraping sound as a chair was pulled up to the bedside.

Reluctantly, Sara took her head out of the pillow and regarded her visitor, who settled herself placidly and said, 'Now, let me introduce myself. I'm Mary McNab —Doctor Mary McNab, but not a medical doctor, I hasten to add. I'm a research biologist. This is a research hospital, by the way, the best in the country. I'm here to work on a special project, but they roped me in to help because it seems you've been posing a bit of a problem to them and they think a fellow-countrywoman might do a bit better.' She grinned and added, 'If you'll accept a Scot as a fellow-countrywoman, that is. Now then, Sara, what's it all about? Why don't you co-operate to get yourself better? Refusing to eat isn't going to help, you know, it'll only make everything worse. They tell me there's nothing physically wrong with you now except the remains of the bruises, and that there's no reason why you shouldn't leave hospital in a day or two, if you'll pull yourself together.'

Sara's eyes flew wide. 'Leave? But I can't, I've nowhere to go.'

Light brown eyes met her own with shrewd kindness. 'Well, we'll come to that later. Look, Sara, is there anything you want to talk about? Anything you want to ask? They've told me about your case, my dear, and I know you lost your husband in that train accident. I know, quite literally, how you feel, because the same thing happened to me not so very long ago. Only it was a plane crash.'

'Oh!' Sara gave a small gasp.

Dr McNab looked out through the window. 'Yes, it's hell for a while, I know.' After a moment she turned back. 'You may not believe me just now, my dear, but life *is* worth living, and anyway you've got to go on living, so you may as well make the best of it, because it's the only life you've got.'

Almost against her will, Sara began to feel a mild interest in her visitor. The practical words, spoken in that crisp, musical voice, shook her from her apathy more than any soft sympathy would have done.

'You've had a rotten time, and a bad shock,' Dr McNab went on, 'and it was made worse by the stupid mistake that was made when your brother-in-law came to see you. I heard all about that. I suppose it was understandable—the name being the same, apparently the reception clerk got mixed up and assumed that Mr Knight was your husband. It was a very hurtful thing for you and it shouldn't have happened. They're most apologetic about it. Mr Knight himself is sorry too, I'm sure. He has called frequently, but they thought it better not to let him see you until you were feeling able to talk to him.'

Sara shrank back in the bed. 'I don't want to see him. He hates me. He blames me for what happened to Tim.'

The cheerful face looked shocked. 'Oh no, I'm sure you're wrong about that. Nobody could possibly blame you. It was the worst rail accident they've had for years and you might so easily have been killed yourself, you know. You were one of the lucky ones.'

'Was I?' said Sara bleakly.

The red-haired doctor took her hand and held it tightly. 'I promise you you'll believe that one day,' she said. 'Look, I'll give you my address in Edinburgh and a year from now you can come and tell me that I was right.' She scribbled on the pad on the bedside locker.

She stood up. 'Mr Knight is waiting now. Shall I ask him to come in?'

'Now? He's here now?' Sara's voice rose in panic. She looked wildly round the room at the other occupants, who were all busy with their own visitors. 'Send him away—please send him away. He—he——'

'Yes?'

'He frightens me,' admitted Sara, and felt her eyes fill with tears.

Dr McNab sat down again. 'H'm—yes, I thought that might be part of the trouble. I've met Mr Knight and I admit he's rather a tough guy.' She grinned at the term. 'But you mustn't let people crush you, Sara. You're a person in your own right and you've got a lot going for you. You're very, very pretty and you really don't need to worry what anyone thinks about you, you know.' There was a gleam of humour in the shrewd brown eyes. 'Especially men,' she added.

She leaned nearer to the bed. 'Don't forget, will you—you need to hold your own in this world, and certainly don't let Mr Knight bully you.'

Looking at that firm, attractive face Sara felt as if she were seeing light at the end of the dark tunnel. It was extraordinary—it was as if life was suddenly flowing back into her. She could feel it all through her body, warm and strong. *I'm myself*, she thought, and the words acted like a sparkling glass of champagne.

Come to think of it, all her life she had relied on others, done as she was told. At school—travelling with Ralph—even when Tim had stepped in and taken charge of her—she had never really had to make her own decisions.

She pulled herself up in bed and for the first time she realised that she had no pain at all when she moved.

She lifted her head high and that wasn't aching either. 'You're right,' she said, 'you're so right about everything. Thank you for coming to see me. And—and will you ask my brother-in-law to come in, please.'

The door had scarcely closed behind Dr McNab when it opened again to admit the pretty young nurse with the brown face and the white smile. She was using the smile now, to great advantage, upon the man beside her.

Immediately Jason Knight came into the small ward all conversation ceased and the eyes of every woman in the room were turned upon the tall, tough, broad-shouldered man who wore his arrogant masculinity with a careless air. He was conventionally dressed today in dark trousers and a white shirt. He even wore a tie. But you would never have mistaken him for a man who spent his life sitting behind a desk, thought Sara, with a tightening of her stomach muscles as he came towards her. With a flash of memory she heard Ralph's words again. The Mexican men were extremely *macho*, he had warned her, and that meant virile—sexually competent. It wasn't only the Mexican men, thought Sara. This man was odiously aware of his own charisma as his narrowed glance passed round the room, without haste.

The other patients and their visitors all looked away and resumed their conversation with renewed vivacity, while Sara waited for him to reach her bedside, trying to relax the tension that was gripping her whole body like a giant hand.

The pretty young nurse pulled out the chair that Dr McNab had replaced against the wall, flashing her smile at Jason Knight, saying something in Spanish which he appeared to understand, for he nodded and replied in the same language. The nurse withdrew somewhat reluctantly and he sat down and turned an unsmiling face towards Sara.

'They tell me you've been sitting out of bed today, and that you're better.'

'Yes, thank you.' With an effort she forced herself to meet his eyes and it was like looking down into a deep well, whose cold depths could only be guessed at with dread. Desperately she hung on to what Dr McNab had said to her: *You mustn't let yourself be crushed.* 'It was kind of you to come and see me,' she managed to add.

His mouth twisted. It was a long mouth, the lips thin and mobile, and it seemed to belie the rest of his features. A mouth like that should smile easily, but it wasn't smiling now. 'I'm sure you don't believe that,' he said. 'You ought to know by now that kindness isn't a weakness of mine where you're concerned.'

He looked away from her as if he couldn't even bear the sight of her and went on implacably, 'Frankly, there's nothing I'd like better than to wash my hands of you completely, but I realise that's impossible. You married my brother, which means that I have a responsibility towards you, whether I like it or not. What I intend to do is to discharge that responsibility as quickly as possible, so that I can put you out of my life for good.'

She managed to keep her eyes fixed steadily on him. It might help if she could think of him as someone without any personal concern with her—a bank manager or a lawyer. A prosecuting counsel, perhaps. Yes, that was it—a man from whom you wouldn't expect understanding, or sympathy, or kindness. A man who took your guilt for granted.

'Yes,' she said tonelessly. 'I accept that that's your wish.'

His eyes turned back quickly and his dark brows raised themselves a fraction. 'I'll come to the point, then, and perhaps we needn't meet again, which I'm sure would be desirable for both of us.'

'That suits me,' she said.

He took a card from his wallet and placed it on the locker. 'That will give you my address in England. Until I get back and can see my lawyer I've no clear idea of what the legal position is.'

Sara frowned. 'Legal position?'

His lip curled. 'Don't let's waste time pretending that isn't what's on your greedy little mind,' he said contemptuously, 'but I'm afraid I can't satisfy your curiosity at this moment. I'm not even sure whether my brother had made a will or not, but as his widow, of course, I imagine you'll want to press your claim against his estate to the limit.'

She said faintly, 'I don't know anything about—about wills, and things like that——'

'No? You surprise me. But if you don't I'm sure the details won't have escaped your stepfather. I'll be back in England shortly,' he went on, ignoring her little gasp. 'I suggest you give me three weeks from now; then if you or your stepfather will contact me I'll put you in touch with my solicitor, who will give you the information you require. Is that clear?' He stood up. 'I hope you'll soon be completely recovered,' he said indifferently, and turned away.

'Please—please don't go.' Sara's mind was spinning and the words seemed to come of their own accord as she realised that this man was all that stood between her and a situation she didn't care to think about.

He turned. 'I don't think there's any more to be said.'

'Yes, there is.' The words stumbled out urgently. 'I need some money.'

He stood looking down at her. 'Yes, I thought I should hear that sooner or later, but I'm afraid you're out of luck, my girl. You won't get a cent until my brother's estate is settled. You'll have to fall back on that stepfather of yours for the moment. Too bad!' he taunted.

She braced herself with a tremendous effort. 'You've made it quite clear that you hate me,' she said, 'but you're Tim's brother and I don't believe you're a man who would leave a girl entirely alone in a foreign country, without friends or relatives or money. Especially as I can't speak a word of the language,' she added, twisting her head away as she fought against treacherous tears.

He sat down again. 'Is that the truth?'

'Yes.' She stared back into his face, struggling for composure.

For what seemed ages he studied her face. 'Eyes like dew-drenched violets!' he observed in a withering tone. 'Was that how you looked at my brother when you conned him into marrying you? I've no doubt you can turn on the tears to order, like the good little actress you are.'

'*Don't let him crush you*,' she told herself desperately. She said in a low voice, 'Do you *have* to be so beastly to me?'

There was a long silence. Then he said expressionlessly, 'I've just come from my brother's funeral. What do you expect?'

'Oh!' Sara gave a little moan and buried her face in her hands, sobbing silently.

The tears went on and on. Sara hadn't cried since Tim's death and now nothing could stop her. She lay face down in her bed, her whole body heaving, convulsed with sobs. When, finally, the tumult of weeping stopped she felt the arm of the Sister sturdily around her, raising her head to drink something warm and soothing from a mug.

'You cry, you better now.' She nodded, smiling. 'You 'ave what you call a good cry.'

Sara smiled back tremulously. The Sister was a good

soul and she was trying to be kind, but oh, if it were
only as easy as that!

'My—Mr Knight has left?'

'*Si*. He say he come back tomorrow.'

To taunt her and torment her again? Was there no
end to it?

Before she slept that night Sara drank a bowl of hot
soup. The nurses were delighted that she was eating
again, and she herself was surprised that the soup tasted
so delicious.

Next morning she ate the breakfast they brought her
and afterwards walked for the first time to the bathroom for her bath. She enjoyed that too; at least the
little things of life were beginning to have meaning
again.

Soon afterwards it was time for the specialist's round.
He stood beside Sara's bed, surrounded by his group of
acolytes, a tall, thin man with bristling grey hair and a
face like a sad bloodhound, with its heavy jowl and
thick-lidded eyes. But he looked kind.

'And how do you feel today, *señora*?' He spoke good
English.

'Better, thank you, much better.' Sara was surprised
to find that it was true. Yesterday had been utterly
traumatic, but it seemed to have left her with a revived
will to live.

He looked gratified. '*Muy bien*. Shall I look at those
bruises now?'

When the examination was over there was an ex-
change of question and answer with the Sister in attend-
ance. The words '*el Señor Knight*' seemed to crop up
frequently and Sara wished she could understand what
they were saying.

The specialist turned back to her. 'You have been
lucky, *señora*. Shock, bruises, a bump to the head—

nothing worse. We need not keep you with us any longer. You will do better now if you return to normal life.'

Sara saw the sympathy in the sad brown eyes. He knew of the accident, of course, and he knew about Tim. But there was no point in explaining to him that she had no normal life now. No real life of any kind to go back to.

'Sister tells me that your brother-in-law is in touch with the hospital and will be looking after you at present,' he went on. 'As that is the case there is no reason why you should not leave the hospital tomorrow. May I wish you good luck, *señora?'*

He patted her shoulder kindly and turned to the next patient.

Jason Knight returned later that day, when Sara was sitting up beside her bed. He drew up a chair and said, without preamble, 'Now, suppose we continue our conversation where we left off yesterday?'

True to her resolve, she met his eyes without flinching. He was dressed more casually today, in navy trousers and a cotton bush-jacket, and he looked, if possible, even tougher, she thought. 'Very well,' she said coolly. 'Where did we leave off? I don't remember.'

'You were telling me, very touchingly, that you're alone in the world, homeless and penniless. I was supposed to have my heart wrung with pity, wasn't that the idea?'

'Not at all,' she said. 'I wouldn't attempt the impossible. You've already told me you have no kindness towards me, so I shouldn't expect pity.'

'Just as well!' he said grimly. 'What exactly *do* you expect, then?'

Sara looked down at her hands, resting on the white cotton gown she had been lent, and was pleased to see that they were quite steady. 'I expect the same treatment that you would, presumably, give to any other member of your family who found herself alone, without any possessions, in a foreign country.'

'And that is?' His face was inscrutable and she wondered if he was preparing to refuse any request from her, if he would really take his bitterness as far as that.

She said in a low voice, 'I hate having to ask you for anything. If there were anyone else I could turn to, I would. But there isn't.'

They regarded each other in tense hostility for a long moment. Then he said, 'Where's your stepfather? Why can't you go back to him?'

'I don't know where he is, or where he was going when he left the hotel at Acapulco. I imagine he will have left by now, but I haven't enquired and I don't want to. I'—her voice shook a little—'I shan't be seeing him again.'

'Until you've collected the loot, is that it?' he mocked.

'I shan't be seeing him again,' she repeated steadily. 'As I told you, I'm entirely alone here. If I can get back to England I'll try to find someone there to help me. My old headmistress, perhaps.' Yes, she thought, with a flicker of hope, Miss Glyn would help her to get into some training course—to get a job, possibly. She had been annoyed and disapproving when Ralph had taken Sara away from school in the year of the A-levels. 'A waste of your education! All these years at school and nothing to show for it!'

Sara had been just turned seventeen then, and dazzled by the exciting life that lay promisingly before her, and she couldn't have cared less about A-levels. It wouldn't be easy to go back and beg for help, but she would do it. She would do anything rather than be in Jason Knight's debt. She said, 'If you'll lend me enough money to buy some clothes to see me through, and to pay my fare back to England, I promise to repay it as soon as I possibly can.'

Jason Knight was regarding her narrowly. 'You know, in spite of everything, you interest me. I don't believe a word of your story, but I've got to take a chance on it simply because Tim married you, God help him. But I warn you, I don't like being fooled.' The strange eyes narrowed. 'If you and that precious stepfather are trying some game on with me you're going to find yourselves on the losing side.'

Sara found herself held by that look, unable to move, just as if he were holding her with those steel-hard hands. She said nothing.

'Do I gather,' he said, 'that you have no clothes with you?'

'Only what I was—was wearing,' she said, very low. That reminded her unbearably of Tim saying, 'We'll get you something pretty to wear in Veracruz,' and her mouth began to tremble.

'Oh, for God's sake don't turn on the tears again,' said Tim's brother. 'It sickens me.'

She wanted to shout at him, to scream, 'And you sicken me, you're inhuman—vindictive——' But she was uncomfortably aware of the sidelong glances they were getting from the other patients in the ward.

He said shortly, 'It seems you're going to be discharged from here tomorrow. I'll get you something to wear and leave it at the reception office. Then you can wait until I come.' He took out a notebook and pen. 'Size in shoes?'

She told him and he scribbled it down. 'The rest I can guess, I imagine.' His glance travelled contemptuously over her, sitting there in the flimsy cotton gown, and she felt her colour rise, as if he had stripped it from her. 'I have an unfortunately vivid recollection of your

charms, as displayed in Acapulco.' He got to his feet and
the way he was looking at her sent shivers through her.
She might have been a slave-girl, on sale at a Roman
market, and he a disdainful patrician, weighing up her
possibilities.

Then, without another word, he nodded brusquely
and walked out of the ward.

The new clothes arrived next morning. The large, amiable Sister who spoke a little English brought in several
colourful and exclusive-looking carriers and put them on
Sara's bed. '*El* Señor Knight, 'e bring them. He return *a
las diez de la mañana*. You put on the clothes, *si*?'

'*Las diez*?' Sara wrinkled her brow.

The Sister clicked her tongue goodnaturedly. 'Ten of
the morning. You 'urry, *señora*. *El* Señor Knight say he
do not wish to wait.'

Sara pursed her lips, wondering if she dared keep him
waiting, just to prove that she wasn't afraid of him.
Would defiance do any good? No, she decided, it
wouldn't have the slightest effect on his attitude to her,
except, perhaps, to make it even more relentlessly hos-
tile.

She sighed and began to unpack the carriers. What
would he have bought for her to wear? she wondered.
Sackcloth and ashes?

The contents of the carriers were a surprise. Nothing
could have been further from sackcloth and ashes than
the exquisite little number in crisp white cotton, double-
layered and with a dark red suede belt. There were red
patent high-heeled sandals and handbag to match.
Swathed in tissue, in another carrier, she found panties
and bras—little bits of white nothing that slid through her
fingers; a selection of hose; a nightie in pleated black silk
with a camisole top; even a box of handkerchiefs em-

broidered in red and black with tiny birds and leaves, intertwined in a Maya design.

The other women in the ward, with whom Sara had by now reached the stage of exchanging smiles and nods, exclaimed with squeaks of admiration as each new piece was unpacked, and by the time Sara was dressed they were surveying her with almost maternal pride and approval. She wondered how much they knew of her circumstances. Not much, probably, the nurses were all too busy to spend time gossiping, and the language barrier had—luckily—stood between her and any personal questions.

There was no mirror in the room, except the tiny one in her original large handbag, which had evidently survived the accident and had been placed on the bedside locker. She took her comb from it and combed out her hair, which must have been washed at some time when she was taking no interest in the proceedings. It smelled faintly of antiseptic, but she wasn't going to let that worry her. It certainly wouldn't lower her standing with Jason Knight; that could hardly be more abysmal than it was already. Her make-up case was in her handbag too, but she decided against putting anything on her face, not even eye-shadow or lipstick. She was clean and tidy and that was all that was required of her. Once she had got away from that man and was safely on a plane bound for England, she could begin to think about facing life again, of taking an interest in all the ordinary little things. She hoped fervently that he had been able to book a flight for her today. He probably had. He had that particular air of authority about him that impresses booking clerks and head waiters. He must have made an insufferable elder brother all these years. No wonder poor Tim had needed to assert his independence!

The Sister put her head round the door, gesturing to

Sara. '*El* Señor Knight is 'ere, *señora*. You come?'

Sara gestured goodbye to her fellow-patients in the ward, and tried a doubtful, '*Adiós*,' which was greeted by a chorus which she took to be an expression of goodwill and encouragement. There were still plenty of nice people around, she thought, as she went out to join one person who was anything but nice.

He was standing just outside the door, very big and impressive in his dark blue pants and shirt, towering above the plump nursing Sister. She was laughing at something he had just said and he was smiling down at her. That smile gave Sara quite a shock; the man looked almost human when he smiled. The long, mobile mouth curved persuasively, and a faint cleft showed in his firm square chin.

He saw her and the smile disappeared. 'You ready, Sara?' The casual way he spoke her name for the first time made her quiver inside and the extraordinary thought flitted through her mind: If only things had been different! If only Tim hadn't been killed and his brother had come to understand her position and accept her as a friend! She pushed the thought away. The accident must have left her weak in the mind, she thought ruefully. This man would never be her friend, never in a million years.

'I'm quite ready,' she said, and turned to thank the Sister for her kindness and that of the other nurses. She wished she could have bought them something—some little present to show her gratitude. Then she saw that the Sister was holding a large, shiny flat box, tied with a bow of satin ribbon. '*Muchas gracias*,' she beamed at them both with pleasure. 'It is most kind.' Then the plump face became sober as she spoke rapidly in Spanish to Jason Knight.

'What was she saying?' asked Sara a moment or two

later, when they were walking together down the long corridor towards the hospital entrance.

He stared straight ahead and his face had its closed, harsh look. 'She expressed her sympathy to us both in our loss and said that God healed all wounds.'

'Oh!' whispered Sara, and they didn't speak again until they were outside the hospital.

'I have a car waiting,' he said, and gripped her arm to lead her across the hospital forecourt. She wondered if he knew the strength of his own hand, and if he intended the hurt he was causing. Wincing, she began to feel like a prisoner in custody, being led off to unknown horrors.

They arrived at the waiting car and he bundled her in unceremoniously and got in beside her. He spoke to the dark-skinned driver with the large straw hat, and Sara caught the word *aeropuerto*. That must mean airport. Surely, she thought, he wasn't going to put her straight on a plane for England? It might be the height of the season in Mexico, and the thin white cotton dress he had bought her was perfect when the sun was pouring down, as it was here. But it was, after all, February, and she must have something warmer to wear for when she stepped out of the plane at Heathrow, or she would look very silly indeed, and feel perished.

She glanced at the impassive face of the man beside her, as the car threaded its way through the traffic. 'Thank you for supplying me with some clothes,' she said, 'but I'm afraid I can't fly back without taking a warm jacket of some sort to wear when I reach England.'

He brushed the words aside with a shrug. 'That'll sort itself out,' he said, and leaned forward to speak to the driver.

Sara said no more on the subject. It was plain that he wasn't going to consider her comfort, and she had no intention of arguing or pleading. He would, presumably, give her some money before he put her on the plane, and she would just have to make for the nearest London store as soon as she arrived, and hope it wasn't snowing or freezing.

The airport was enormous, noisy and confusing. Sara was accustomed to airports and she had always left the arrangements to Ralph. Now, amid the din and bustle, and the unintelligible voices over the public address loudspeakers, she left everything to Jason Knight and followed him without question, secure in the knowledge that he was—as he had said—just as anxious to part company from her as she was from him.

The preliminaries over, he joined her and said, 'Only a short wait. Do you want a coffee or anything?'

'No, thank you,' said Sara, as they made their way to the departure lounge. He indicated a seat, but Sara shook her head. She felt keyed up and tense, waiting for the moment when she would be away from this intimidating man and be able to breathe freely again. He stood beside her, not speaking, his eyes following the moving, drifting crowd of people without interest.

The loudspeaker came echoingly across the lounge. 'Ah, here we go then. Come along,' said Jason Knight, leading the way to the barrier.

Sara hung back a bit. She said, 'I haven't any money at all. I told you——' Once through the barrier she was on her own and she couldn't face arriving in England with only a few pesos in her purse. She had never handled money when she was with Ralph; he only allowed her enough for the occasional coffee or chemist's expenses.

'You won't need any now,' said Jason Knight impatiently. 'Come *on*, we don't want to hang around.'

It was then that Sara realised the truth that her muddled state of mind had concealed from her. He had never had the faintest intention of sending her back to England.

They were through the barrier now and walking down the long catwalk. Jason Knight was still beside her. In the moving stream of passengers she could do nothing but go where he took her, and anyway his hand was gripping her arm again, which was beginning to feel sore and bruised where his fingers dug into it.

'Where are we going?' she asked in a small voice. He didn't hear, or pretended not to, for he made no reply, merely urged her forward. Sara shrugged and gave it up. Without money she was helpless to resist. Dr McNab had advised her not to let herself be crushed. What, she thought now, would be Dr McNab's advice on *this* situation?

The plane was airborne before any further words were exchanged between them. Sara loosened her seat-belt and looked around. The cabin was full; every seat was occupied. She glanced up at the man sitting beside her, frowning over some papers he had taken from his briefcase.

She said, 'Am I allowed to ask where you're taking me?'

He flipped over a couple of sheets of paper, apparently searching for something, ignoring her words. Then he evidently found what he wanted, for he deliberately replaced the sheets in order. Not until then did he turn to her. 'Certainly,' he said calmly. 'We're bound for the Yucatan. To Cancún Island, which, to be precise isn't an island at all. In case you don't happen to know it, it's one of the newer of the resorts. It's been developed within the last few years. I have business there. Actually,

I was on my way there when my journey had to be'—
there was a long pause and his eyes went hard and bleak
—'postponed.'

Sara said under her breath, 'When you took me to the
airport I thought I was flying back to England.'

'I said nothing about your flying back to England.' He
was looking hard at her now.

'But you knew that was what I wanted.'

He smiled thinly. 'But you see, I happened to want
something different. I intend to keep you with me, to
keep an eye on you, until we both return to England
together, as you seem so keen on going there. I take it
that your stepfather has already arranged a rendezvous
with you there?'

She drew in a furious breath. 'I told you already—I'm
not seeing him again—ever.'

'And I,' he returned calmly, 'don't believe you. But
I mean to know the truth.'

She had to restrain herself with a terrific effort from
striking out at him physically, as she had done before, in
Acapulco. No other person in all her life had managed to
rouse such intense, seething anger in her.

When she could control herself she glanced round at
the other passengers and said in a low, shaking voice, 'I
think you should have warned me.'

'And have you bursting into crocodile tears, or having
hysterics on me? You do that sort of thing very convincingly. I suppose it's all part of your stock in trade?'

'Oh!' she gasped, and under her breath she hissed, 'I
think you're the most hateful, despicable, contemptible
man I've ever known!'

The dark brows rose a fraction. 'Really? Well, perhaps
you'll excuse me if I get on with some work during the
flight as our conversation isn't exactly of a very high
standard.' He fished in his briefcase and drew out an

illustrated magazine. 'Would you care to amuse yourself
with this—and I expect there'll be some coffee round
soon.'

She took the magazine. He was putting on a courteous
act for the benefit of the other passengers within ear-
shot. That only made him more detestable, she thought,
and she turned her back on him and stared at the cot-
tonwool clouds drifting past the window with a feeling
of utter and complete desolation.

## CHAPTER FOUR

THE hotel on Cancún Island, when they finally arrived
there after the drive from the airport, was a surprise to
Sara. She had expected one of the magnificent white
giants with sea views from every window, such as they
had stayed at in Acapulco, but the taxi drew up before
a businesslike building in the centre of what appeared
to be a modern city.

The entrance lounge was furnished in comfortable
brown leather. There were one or two potted palms
and the pictures on the walls were obviously of Mexican
scenes, but there was no white marble; no splashing
fountains; no drifting, laughing, bikini-clad holidayers.
Only a couple of men sat at one of the glass-topped
tables, talking earnestly over their tall beer glasses.

'This is Ciudad de Cancún,' Jason said as they entered.
'The planners have built modern apartment blocks and
offices here to house the personnel who service the resort part of the island. And I bet it takes a lot of hard
work to keep the wheels turning in a place like Cancún, from what I've heard of it.'

'You haven't been here before?'

He shook his head. 'I only know that it promises big business for my firm if things go right. I've got an appointment with one of the top men later this afternoon and a lot hangs on that. I'm afraid I shall have to leave you to look after yourself.'

'I'll be all right,' she said swiftly. It would be a relief to be alone.

He shot her a hard, suspicious look and went over to the reception desk. She watched him as he talked to the woman behind the counter. Even his back looked resolute, self-sufficient, as if he knew exactly what he was doing. Sara sighed and wished fervently that *she* did.

He came back, jingling the room keys, and they went up in a lift to the second floor and along a passage to a door at the end. Sara glanced round the smallish room, plainly furnished in a modern style with lightwood fitments. There was a double bed covered with a cotton quilt in Mayan design. The room had all the amenities and it looked clean and comfortable. She walked across to the window and looked down on the street below. In the heat of the early afternoon the street was drowsy and lazy, with little moving about. A large dog lay panting in the comparative shade of a house doorway opposite.

Behind her, Jason remarked in the ironic tone that he seemed to have chosen to speak to her, 'I'm afraid this is a bit of a comedown from the Plaza-International in Acapulco. I trust madam will be comfortable. *Not* air-conditioned, but a ceiling fan is provided.' He switched it on and a comforting cool breeze whirred into the room.

Sara turned from the window. 'Oh, that's lovely! I'm so *hot*.' She sank on to the bed. She was tired too; she hadn't realised how tired until this minute. The first hours after her leaving hospital had hardly been calculated to relax and soothe. 'I think I'd like to sleep, if that's all right with you.'

He shrugged. 'Perfectly. But don't you want lunch?'

'No, thanks.' She sank back against the pillows. Her eyelids were so heavy that she could hardly keep them open. She wished he would go away so she could slip into oblivion.

But he seemed to be hesitating, standing beside the bed, looking down at her limp body in the white cotton dress. Then he said, more brusquely than ironically, 'You'll be dehydrated if you don't have something to drink. You've had nothing since that coffee on the plane.' He glanced towards the wash-basin and grimaced. '*Not* the water, I think. I'll bring you a bottle of something.'

She was half asleep when he came back. 'Here, drink this.' He held out a tall glass to her.

'Thank you,' she whispered, and made an effort to sit up as she took the glass, spilling some of the contents on her dress.

Jason clicked his tongue. 'Here, give it to me.' He took the glass from her and slipped a hand round her back, raising her from the bed. The feeling of his hand, through the thin dress, gave her the most extraordinary sensation. Her flesh tingled where his fingers pressed into it and in her exhausted state she felt as if some strange magnetism were passing from his body to hers. He was her enemy, she thought confusedly, and his touch should have been hateful to her, but when she had drunk the cool lime-flavoured contents of the glass and he lowered her to the bed again and took his hand away, she wanted to cry.

Her eyes swam with weak tears, so that the sight of

him, standing above her, was blurred and hazy, and the long mobile mouth looked almost kind. If only he would treat her as a human being, she thought, how much more bearable everything would be. Perhaps if she waited, if she were patient, he might begin to see her in a more reasonable light.

'Jason,' she whispered. 'Couldn't—couldn't we be— friends?'

Through the tears that clouded her eyes she could see his face change. 'Dear God,' he breathed savagely, 'what sort of a woman are you?'

He swung away and strode out of the room, closing the door behind him with a vicious slam.

Sara turned her head into the pillow. It was no good, she thought helplessly, he didn't intend to forgive her. However unfair it was, he blamed her for Tim's death, and no appeal to reason or justice was going to make any difference, so she would just have to make the best of it until he took her back to England and she could get away from him.

It didn't matter, she told herself, she was too tired to worry about anything. Her eyes closed and she slept.

She must have been asleep for hours and she wakened clear-eyed and feeling better physically than she could have believed possible. The fan was still whirring away in the ceiling, but the room felt warm with the accumulated heat of the day. She glanced at her watch and saw that it was nearly six o'clock.

Swinging her legs off the bed, she looked ruefully down at the white dress she was still wearing, which was very much the worse for wear by now, all its earlier crispness gone. With a spurt of vindictiveness utterly foreign to her she decided that if Jason Knight were determined to trail her round with him—to 'keep an eye on her' as he put it, though she couldn't imagine why he should want to—then he would have to dip into his pocket a little further and provide her with at least one more dress.

She felt hot and sticky. It would be lovely to have a shower, but she didn't relish the idea of wandering round a strange hotel looking for a bathroom, and it didn't look the kind of place to provide much in the way of room service. So the wash-basin in the corner would have to do.

Pulling off her dress, she splashed cool water over her face and arms and dried on the small hand-towel. She draped the limp white dress over a chair beside the open window in the hope of freshening it up and then sat down before the mirror to comb her hair. She peered at her reflection with the first spark of interest for some time and decided that she looked a wreck. She also realised that she was feeling hungry and wondered how she could find some food. As she had refused lunch, it would be just like Jason Knight's nasty temper to make her wait until dinner time—which, she had found, could be anything, in Mexico, from eight o'clock until midnight.

At least she could do something about her face. She took her little make-up box from her handbag and set to work, combing out her golden hair into some sort of shape. It really wouldn't look decent again until she had washed it, or visited a hairdresser, but it might have been worse. She sprayed some toilet cologne over it hoping to mask the smell of the antiseptic they had used in hospital.

Her tan had faded a little during the days in bed, and her skin had lost some of its silky smoothness, due, no doubt, to shock. There wasn't much she could do about that, but she smoothed moisturiser over her cheeks, decided against using colour and compromised by a shine of eye-shadow and just a touch of mascara on the long curving lashes that fringed the huge, shadowed violet eyes that stared back at her.

'You look like a ghost,' she said aloud, in disgust, picking up a lipstick.

'Or a siren,' said Jason Knight's dry voice from the opposite side of the room.

Sara spun round on the stool to see him standing in the doorway, leaning nonchalantly against the frame, his eyes fixed on her unsmilingly.

'Oh!' she gasped. How long had he been standing there watching her? The whirring of the ceiling fan must have made her unaware that the door had been opened. She was uncomfortably aware that she was wearing nothing but gossamer panties and a minuscule bra, and that her heart was thumping against her ribs.

She reached hastily for her dress. 'You might have knocked or something,' she said crossly.

He sauntered across the room and took the dress out of her hands. 'I'm not in the habit of knocking at the door of my own room,' he said calmly.

'*Your* room?' Sara gasped. 'Then why——' Her eyes travelled round the room quickly as if she expected to find some dangerous animal hiding in the recesses. What she did see was a small stack of slim air-travel bags standing against the wall in a corner. They could have been there all the time without her noticing them.

'Why are you here?' He took the words from her. 'Why have you been sleeping in *my* bed, as the time-honoured fairy tale has it? Quite simple—a slight problem in the reception office.' His choice of words might have meant that he intended a joke, but he wasn't smiling. In fact, the way he was looking at her, almost naked as she was, sent a tremor of something like fear through her. If she hadn't known how much he hated and despised her it might have been real fear.

'Perhaps you would show me which my room is, then?' she said, and held out her hand. 'May I have my dress, please?'

He tossed the white dress on the bed. 'You won't be needing this again. The saleswoman in Mexico City chose it. I certainly wouldn't have thought of dressing you in virginal white.' His mouth twisted contemptuously. 'I'm sure you'll feel more at home in this.' He walked over to pick up a carrier bag he must have brought in with him. There was a rustle of tissue and he was holding up a wisp of a dress in scarlet chiffon with a sparkle of sequins. 'Sexy little number, don't you think?' He shook out the dress, holding it by the fragile shoulder-straps. 'I rather fancy the idea of being the envy of every man around, with such a luscious lady in tow, when we go out to dinner tonight. Oh, yes'—his glance swept her insolently—'all the fellows will be positively drooling when they see you. But for the moment, my sweet charmer, *I'm* your protector, whether you like it or not.'

Sara cowered back in her chair, crossing her arms over her breast as if she could cover herself up from his scrutiny. 'I—I don't want to come out with you. Can't I have something to eat here, and you can go out to dine on your own?'

He lounged back against the door, smiling thinly, barring her way as if he expected her to make a bolt for it. 'Oh, but surely you won't deny me the pleasure of your company? I'm sure we shall have so much in common to discuss, now that we're so closely related.'

Angry tears stung her eyes. 'Why do you have to be like this?' she choked out. 'Why can't you just send me back to England and then you won't have to bother with me any more? What pleasure can you possibly get out of this—this cat and mouse game you're playing?'

The strange, clay-coloured eyes seemed to darken. He went on staring at her, but now she thought that he was hardly seeing her at all. For the first time she saw in his face not anger but grief, stark and naked.

Then he moved his shoulders, turning his head away. 'I could use you as an opiate,' he said indifferently. 'A drug to assuage the pain.'

Her inside began to shake. Suddenly she remembered the words she thought she had heard him say when he turned away from her in the hospital : 'And, by God, I'll make you pay!' Memory took her back again to the poolside in Acapulco, when he had first tackled her about her friendship with Tim. She remembered how he had towered over her, the blue cotton shirt hanging open to disclose the powerful muscles of his shoulders, the lean brown chest with the tangle of dark hair. She remembered how the sheer size and power of the man had made her feel weak and defenceless. But then there had been people around; then he had been no threat to her; then he had had no reason to seek revenge. Now everything was different. She was alone with him in this room; he could do what he liked with her. Her eyes flicked towards the big double bed and sheer terror gripped her.

She must keep her head, she thought sickly. Above all, she mustn't let him see how frightened she was. Her first impulse had been to fight him with all her strength, to resist all along the line anything he intended to make her do. But that wouldn't be any good; her puny strength would be as nothing against the whipcord of those arms and that body. He could use her in any way he chose.

He was standing above her now, and to her fevered

imagination the strange clay-coloured eyes had a glint of anticipation; he looked like a great jungle cat, very still in the undergrowth, watching his prey with every sense alert, enjoying the moments before the final swift leap.

He came towards her, holding the scarlet dress out. 'Put it on,' he ordered.

She stared at the filmy bit of nothing in his hand and knew he had chosen it to make her look like a—a tart. 'I won't wear that,' she said. 'I won't come out with you, to be taken as your——'

'*Fille de joie?*' he sneered. 'I can't say I've had much joy out of your acquaintance up to now. All the same'— his tone was like the cut of a whip—'you *will* wear it, and you *are* coming out with me.'

Before she knew what he meant to do, he had pulled her up out of the chair and slipped the scarlet dress over her head, just as if she were a racehorse reluctant to enter the stalls and he was throwing a blindfold over her.

Panic seized her, an hysteria born of all that she had been through in the last awful days. She threshed out desperately with arms and legs, fighting against the choking red darkness of the folds of chiffon enclosing her head, sucking into her mouth like a gag. Then the horror was over as quickly as it had begun. Jason's knees had closed round her legs, holding her impotent while he gripped her flailing hands with one of his own great hands, and pulled the dress down with the other. Her face was free.

As she ceased to struggle he let go of her hands and she gripped the bottom rail of the old-fashioned bedstead. Her limbs had turned to jelly and she felt as if she might collapse in a huddle on the floor at any moment.

He smoothed the dress over her body, his hands lingering on her smooth skin: on the hollow of her back, on the curve round her firm young breasts to her waist, down her hips and thighs. She turned her head away from him, biting into her lip to try to control the shudders that were rising through her body at the touch of his hands—terrifying and yet in some dreadful way exciting too.

'There!' He stood away from her at last. 'Very classy! Cancún's really an up-and-coming spot. Lots of snazzy little boutiques to tempt the tourist; one doesn't have to settle for the locally-made *huipiles* unless one chooses. But we might get you one before——'

He broke off, staring at her as she sagged against the rails of the bed. 'What's the matter? Are you ill?'

He raised his hand, and instinctively, like a small frightened animal, she cowered away from him. 'Don't —please don't——' she moaned.

'Don't what?' he rasped.

'Don't hurt me—please don't. I can't take any more —I'll——'

'Hurt you?' The angry amazement in his voice was genuine enough. 'What in God's name gave you that idea? I'm no monster, I assure you, I have a sex drive that is quite normal.'

In the silence that followed his words she forced herself to lift her head and look at him and she saw that he was smiling—a grim smile, to be sure, a smile that held no humour but only irony, and a touch of contempt in the twist of the long flexible mouth. But at least it wasn't a cruel smile and she let out her breath in relief.

'So you see,' he added, 'you needn't start having regrets.'

Regrets? she thought, muddledly. What did he mean

—regrets? But she wasn't going to ask him; she wasn't going to make any more of a fool of herself than she had done already.

'Come along now,' he said briskly. 'Let's cut out the melodrama. I'm hungry even if you're not. Now, finish doing whatever it was to yourself that you were doing when I came in, while I change.' He lifted one of the slim travel bags on to the bed and unlocked it, tossing out the top layer of its contents. He pulled the cotton shirt he was wearing over his head and unfastened the belt of his pants, letting them slip down to the floor.

Sara sank down on the chair before the mirror again, turning her eyes away from the sight of him, from the powerful bronzed body, naked except for the tight-fitting briefs which only emphasised his masculinity. It was stupid, she told herself, appalled at the way her heart was pounding against her ribs, to react like this. On the sun-baked beaches where she had spent most of the last months, the men wore no more than he was wearing now—sometimes even less—but she had never for a moment experienced the hot flood of awareness that was pulsing through her now.

She picked up her lipstick with trembling fingers and leaned towards the mirror, but his reflection was there too. She said in a small voice, 'Have you found out yet where my room is? I could go along there.'

Their eyes met in the mirror and she was painfully conscious of her flushed cheeks. 'No,' he said. 'I didn't give it a thought—I've had other things on my mind this afternoon. Business matters.' She saw the way his eyes narrowed, his mouth curled into mocking disbelief. 'Surely you're not going to pretend you're embarrassed —that you've never seen a man undress before?'

'As a matter of fact, I haven't,' she said, and then,

summoning up a little show of spirit, 'but as you don't seem to believe anything I say, I don't suppose you'll believe that either.'

He smiled grimly. 'No, I don't.'

He seemed to lose interest in the subject. 'God, it's hot! I'm going to have a shower. There's a bathroom two doors along, by the way, in case you haven't found it.' He picked up a towel and went to the door, pausing before he went out to say, 'I expect you find this place a bit primitive—it's geared for commercial types, not tourists. But you see I didn't expect to be entertaining a lady when I booked the accommodation.'

He went out and closed the door, leaving her to make what she liked of that statement.

There was only one thing she *could* make of it, and the prospect took over her body with a tension that gripped and pulsed through her like physical pain.

She sat motionless before the mirror, staring into wide, frightened eyes, whose deep violet was echoed in the shadows beneath them. Jason Knight believed her to be a—what would he call it?—a tramp. He thought she was sophisticated, sexually experienced. He had lost someone close to him, a loved younger brother, and because he blamed her for that loss he intended to use her quite deliberately to 'assuage the pain', as he put it. He would take her body just as carelessly as another man might drink himself into insensibility.

She tried desperately to think. Somehow she had got to convince him that his picture of her was inaccurate in every detail. That, far from being the kind of woman who would be capable of satisfying him—of acting as a drug, as he had said—she was innocent, callow, naïve, ingenuous, totally ignorant of the arts of love. Somehow she must get him to listen to her, to make him understand. And somehow she must keep a tight hold on her emotions. No more melodrama. She would be quiet, contained, reasonable. She would somehow *make* him believe her. And she wouldn't let herself be crushed—as Dr McNab had put it—by his overpowering masculinity. She would stand up for herself.

She put a little more blusher on her cheeks, blending it up so that the violet shadows beneath her eyes were partly disguised. When Jason came back into the room a few minutes later she was sitting up straight, putting the finishing touches to the silky gold of her hair.

She wouldn't look at his reflection in the mirror, but she knew from the sound that he had tossed away the towel and guessed that he was pulling on briefs and pants.

'You all ready?' he asked from across the room, and she nodded, keeping her back stiff, not trusting her voice.

'You haven't fastened your dress,' he said, coming up behind her. 'There's a short zipper here—keep still and I'll do it for you.' She tried not to wince away as she felt his hands at her back. 'I presume,' he said musingly, 'that this is all that keeps the dress up.' There was a little tug as he manipulated the zipper. 'There, that looks O.K. to me.' There was a pause and he didn't remove his hands. 'Very much O.K.,' he added softly.

Sara held her breath, sitting transfixed as his hands travelled up her back and across the soft hollows in front of her shoulders, to find their way beneath the folds of scarlet chiffon and close gently over her breasts. He bent his head and his mouth burrowed beneath the fall of her hair to bury itself in the nape of her neck. His lips were warm and gentle and as they moved on her skin Sara, to her utmost horror, felt a deeply convulsive shudder pass through her, which couldn't have been unnoticed by him.

When finally he disengaged himself their gazes met in the mirror, hers wide-eyed and shaken, his mocking.

'Payment on account,' he said, and moved away to thrust his arms roughly into the sleeves of a cream-coloured evening shirt. She watched him in the mirror as he fastened the buttons, then she turned in her chair, finding her voice at last. 'Jason, there's something I must tell you—explain to you. I know what you're thinking about me, but I'm not what you think. I'm——'

'*Think* about you?' he broke in harshly. 'I don't *think* about you at all. You're not the kind of girl that men would *think* about. Look at yourself!' With a violent movement he crossed back to her and twisted her round in her chair to face the mirror again. 'Look at yourself, my beautiful little tramp. Hair like sunlight, eyes like drenched violets, skin like flower petals, a mouth——' his eyes fastened on it with a look so explicit that no further words were needed. 'You've got it made, haven't you?' The contempt in his voice bit into her. 'What man with eyes in his head and guts in his body could resist you?' he added crudely. 'My poor Tim certainly couldn't. But *he* offered marriage, didn't he, and your stepfather's pal Sorano didn't. That was how it was, wasn't it? Wasn't it?' He was leaning over her, his hands digging into her shoulders.

'No—no, it wasn't like that at all. You're making it up.'

'I didn't have to make it up. I saw it with my own eyes. I saw you going off to Sorano's house that evening —you all dressed up and ready to move in for the kill, your stepfather positively licking his lips over the prospect of a millionaire son-in-law. Oh, it was all so disgustingly obvious.'

'It wasn't like that at all—you've got it wrong——'

He went on as if she hadn't spoken, the hard, relentless words beating against her brain. 'But Carlos Sorano didn't come up to scratch, did he? He was too wily a bird to be caught like that by a smooth con-man and his glamorous decoy of a stepdaughter. Marriage wasn't in his book. And what he offered for your—favours— wasn't enough to pay the debts your stepfather had run up. So—no deal!'

Sara couldn't take any more. Finding strength in her anger, she twisted out of his grasp and stumbled across the room, putting the width of the bed between them, her hands holding on convulsively to the big brass knob at the corner of the bedstead.

'How dare you?' she flashed at him, all her brave resolution to stay cool and reasonable forgotten. 'You're being unfair. You're just guessing. You don't know the first thing about me, or about Ralph.'

Standing feet apart, hands on hips, he surveyed her flushed face. In his fitting black pants and loose shirt, his rough dark hair swept to one side over his bronzed forehead, his square jaw set in a hard line, he looked a formidable man, a dangerous man. 'Don't I?' he said softly.

She held her ground with an effort. 'No, you don't. How could you?'

His mouth hardened. 'In point of fact, I know several things about Ralph——' he made the name into a sneer. 'One thing is that a very close friend of mine was effectively duped by that same gentleman, a year or two ago when we were both staying in Greece. My friend only narrowly escaped being involved in a criminal case, through no fault of his own. As it was he ended up in the bankruptcy court, and is only now beginning to get his head above water again. We made enquiries and what we found out about Mr Ralph Francis was fairly disgusting and totally damning. But by that time, of course, he'd disappeared into the blue.'

Oh God, thought Sara, that had the ring of truth about it. She remembered how Ralph had kept moving on; leaving places suddenly. If only she had guessed— but how could she?

'He was operating on his own then,' Jason's ruthless voice went on. 'You were a later addition to his bag of tricks.' His contemptuous gaze raked her. 'An eminently marriageable so-called stepdaughter. You can perhaps imagine my joy when I found out who it was that my poor gullible young brother had got himself mixed up with in Acapulco.'

Her mouth was shaking. How could she explain and make him believe her? Part of what he said was so near the truth, the part about Ralph. But the rest of it? 'You're so wrong about some things,' she pleaded. 'I know it looks bad, but won't you let me tell you—let me explain——'

His composure cracked. He took a couple of strides across the room and stood looming over her. 'There's just one thing you can tell me.' His voice was low and menacing. 'Anything else is beside the point. Tell me that you were in love with Tim when you married him.' He put a hand under her chin and raised her face to his. 'Look at me and swear that you were in love with him. I shall know if you're telling the truth or not.'

She stared up into his eyes, held helplessly by the strange, pale light in them. 'I—I——' she stammered. She couldn't say it, couldn't tell him the lie.

With a sound of disgust he threw her away from him and she sank down to the bed, covering her face with her hands. He turned his back and walked to the window and stood looking out. After what seemed a long silence, with only the whirr of the fan, and the voices from the street below combined with the sound of cars and the cries of children, he came back and stood looking down at her, sitting crushed on the bed, like some fragile scarlet flower, all Dr McNab's good advice forgotten.

'Oh, for Pete's sake, girl,' he said wearily. 'Let's forget the high drama. What's done is done. We have to accept the past and live with it, face the situation as it is at present. The situation is that I've made up my mind to keep you under my eye until things are resolved, so that's that.'

The matter-of-factness of his words got through to her in her misery. She lifted her head. 'What things?' she asked.

'Oh, this and that. Come along now, we've wasted enough time. I want my dinner.'

Sara sighed and lifted her head. It was true, what he said, regrets got you nowhere. Nothing she could do would wipe out the past, or bring Tim back. And nothing she could say to this hard, implacable man would convince him that his own version of the situation was not the true one.

'Come *on*, Sara,' he said irritably, holding the door open.

Once again the sound of her name on his lips gave her an odd *frisson*. The scene that had just passed between them seemed to have altered things in a strange kind of way. For the first time in her life she caught a glimpse of the truth that harsh words exchanged between a man and a woman contain their own kind of intimacy.

She reached for the scarlet sandals he had bought her in Mexico City and pulled them on. 'I'm coming,' she said, and followed him out of the room.

Jason helped Sara courteously into the taxi and got in beside her. He spoke to the olive-skinned, black-moustached driver, and then settled back into his corner.

'All right?' he enquired, looking over to Sara with a solicitous smile.

'Yes, thank you,' she said stiffly. Now that they were away from the hotel bedroom he had evidently decided to treat her as his dinner guest, not his despised enemy. She had an uneasy feeling that she would rather he had remained an enemy. If he chose to be charming he might undermine her armour of dislike and resentment. Already she had been aware of the effect that his devastating masculine magnetism could have on her senses. She glanced at him now, lounging back in the car seat, long legs spread nonchalantly, arms crossed behind his dark head, and she wondered, with a sinking feeling inside, what would happen between them before the night was out—how far he intended to go to 'make her pay'. Yes, she resolved, she would need all her strength of will and mind to stand up to him. Determinedly she kept her voice cool, her face tranquil, as she asked, 'Where are we dining?'

With a touch of irony he replied, 'We're heading for the lagoon side now where all the glitter is to be found. The Mexican tourist industry has really poured money into developing Cancún. They spent three years planning it—by computer, believe it or not—as the perfect vacation resort, and now they're cashing in on the investment. Not for nothing did the Maya call it Cancún —which means Pot of Gold.' His long mouth pulled into a wry smile as he added '—which is, incidentally, why I'm here myself. I hope to collect some of the gold.'

'To sell your boats?' Sara enquired. Tim had been very vague about the family business and she knew nothing of the details of the Mexican trip.

Jason gave her a rather hard look. 'Boats—and equipment,' he said. 'I should have thought you'd have found out all about our activities and financial standing.'

'No,' she said, puzzled. 'Why should I?'

He said nothing, his eyes considering her narrowly. Then he shrugged. 'No matter. Look, we're coming into the lush quarter now. Quite something, isn't it?'

Sara nodded, and in spite of everything she felt her spirits rising. Everything was sparkling in the early evening light. The luxury hotels, the tropical gardens spilling over with colour, the beach, pale and palm-laced, and beyond that the almost unbelievably clear blue of the lagoon. Although the heat of the day had passed it was still very warm and some people strolled around in bikinis or swimming trunks, while others were already dressed for the evening entertainment ahead, the girls looking like flowers in their diaphanous dresses, the men in the usual resort wear of pants and loose shirts.

'It's a lovely spot,' said Sara, turning back to Jason with a smile.

'Lovely,' he agreed, his eyes searching her, rather than the view outside the car window. 'Lovely.' He reached forward and put his hand on her thigh.

She felt the blood surge hotly through her body. She was completely out of her depth with a man like this, but she guessed that he moved in a world where a gesture like this would be a compliment rather than a liberty. She slid a sideways glance at him and met his eyes, fixed on her with an expression that made every nerve in her body tingle. All her boarding-school training and upbringing warned her that she should not allow such an intimate caress, but on the other hand she wouldn't want to reject what, to him, was probably a perfectly ordinary gesture of friendship between a man and a girl. Any gesture of friendship from Jason Knight was not to be stifled at birth. Besides, when he kept his hand where it was, she felt a strange and delicious weak-

ness stealing through her limbs and she probably couldn't
have moved away if she had tried.

She swallowed and said, 'Have you—changed your
mind about me?'

He raised an eyebrow, which made him look madden-
ingly enigmatic. 'Let's put it this way,' he said. 'I think
I may have been a little hasty.'

Not wildly encouraging, thought Sara, as the taxi
drew to a halt, but at least he wasn't looking angry still.
If the evening went on as it had begun it would be a
tremendous relief. As he led her into the restaurant, a
hand firm at her elbow, she began to relax for the first
time for many days.

The way into the restaurant led along a path through a
jungle garden. Here and there small tables were set in
little clearings, most of them empty, for it was early in
the evening yet. The path opened on to a wide paved
patio with a huge pot either side of the arched entrance.
From the pots issued a musky, aromatic scent that drifted
away among the trees.

'What is it?' asked Sara, fascinated. For the moment
she forgot who was beside her, and put a hand on Jason's
arm to stop him, while she examined the pots.

'Incense,' he said softly, covering her hand with his
own. 'Heady stuff, isn't it? Guaranteed by the Maya to
rouse the senses—though probably they weren't always
the spiritual ones.' He drew her hand into the crook
of his arm, pressing it intimately against him so that
she felt the warmth of his body through the thin silk
shirt. 'This was all jungle country not so very long ago,
you know. Who knows what grisly secrets might have
been uncovered when they decided to civilise it? Altar
slabs, and so on. They had some rather nasty ways of
treating their beautiful young virgins around these parts,
although the tour operators and their couriers don't ex-

actly dwell on it.' He chuckled deep in his throat as she shivered.

'Let's go in.' said Sara hurriedly, and he laughed again., mocking her.

'Don't let your imagination run away with you, you're quite safe with me.'

*Am I*? Sara thought rather wildly. *Am I really? I don't believe a word of it.* The way he was looking at her now, grey eyes glinting under lowered thick lashes, he looked as if he would sacrifice her to any horrible jaguar god, or whatever, without a qualm. She turned before him into the restaurant.

Inside it was cool and dim, the tables set intimately in separate small alcoves, each covered by its own thatch. Jason stood looking around him. 'Yet another mock-up of a Mayan village.' he observed dryly. 'They certainly know how to cash in on the local colour. But this is nicely done.'

When they had been led to their table by a whitecoated steward who seemed to know Jason's name, he went on, 'I must congratulate my friend Ramón. Ramón Mendez, by the way, is the fellow I've been doing my business with this afternoon. He runs this place as well as the latest marina, and he advised me to dine here.'

Sara looked around her in the light from the candles that stood on each table in decorated pottery holders. More pots and jars stood massed on shelves against the walls, which were hung with woven cloths with spiny star designs in the clear reds and blues and yellows and greens which she was beginning to recognise, now, as the typical Mayan colourings. In the centre of the far wall hung a carved wooden mask with terrifying eyes and teeth and animal hair hanging over its face. An enormous red rose was stuck on the top of its head, which made Jason chuckle again.

'I like the Mexicans,' he said. 'They have a sense of humour to go with their sense of their somewhat brutal past.'

The waiter approached and Jason said, 'I believe baby lobster's the speciality here. All right for you?'

'Thank you,' said Sara. She was realising that she had a schoolgirl appetite. It would have been nice if she could have felt easy with Jason, if she could have sighed, 'Lobster—lovely—I'm absolutely starving!' But she couldn't relax. All the time she felt his eyes on her, probing, judging her, summing her up. So all the time she had to be on her guard, saying nothing and doing nothing that would endanger this slightly more friendly way he was treating her.

He ordered the meal, speaking to the waiter in Spanish, and presently aperitifs were set before them. 'X-Tabentun,' said Jason, and spelt it for her. 'See how you like it. It's a traditional Mayan drink.'

It tasted of aniseed and, after a tentative sip or two, Sara found she did like it. The tiny tamales, stuffed with chicken flavoured with achiote sauce, were delicious. But most delicious of all was the lobster dish that followed. Jason seemed to be enjoying his food, too, and Sara was glad he didn't seem to want to make conversation while they ate. All he did was to draw her attention to the ingredients in the different dishes, and keep filling up her glass with tequila. Soon she was beginning to feel delightfully replete, warm, and not a little hazy, and by the time a dish of fresh fruits was set on the table, with a tall pot of coffee, she felt almost happy, in a strange, unfamiliar way. Jason sat back in his chair, sipping his cognac and regarding her under lowered lashes.

'Temptation!' he said in a voice so deep that its note seemed to reverberate through her head.

'What?' She jumped in surprise.

His mouth twisted. 'You, of course. Temptation personified, in that scarlet dress with the bits of glitter outlining your most charmingly alluring—er—attractions. You've held the eye of every male who's walked in—and don't say you didn't notice.'

She hadn't noticed. She had been too aware of the man sitting opposite to look around, but she did so now and saw that all the other tables were occupied, under their little thatched campies. Somewhere in the shadows a guitar was strumming softly. The dim, intimate candlelight; the gentle twang of the music; the musky scent of incense heavy on the warm evening air; everything here pointed to an atmosphere planned for romance. And Jason Knight must have got the message, for he was making love to her with his eyes, with his voice.

Sara's head reeled. What had happened to change things between them—to alter his attitude to her so completely? She wished she didn't feel so muzzy and that she hadn't drunk so much. She knew that there was something that she should be aware of, but at the moment she was aware of nothing but the narrowed darklashed eyes that looked into hers and the way the long mouth curved. There was danger in this man, but there was fascination too, an excitement that sent a tingle through her nerves.

She was saved from thinking of a reply to his provocative remark when he got to his feet as a man approached their table, a tall, striking-looking man with curly grey hair against his swarthy, wide forehead.

The two men were shaking hands, exchanging greetings in Spanish, which Sara could not understand. The newcomer was gazing at her now, then looking questioningly back to Jason, who said a few words to him and then added to Sara, 'This is Señor Mendez, Sara, I told you about him earlier on.'

Señor Mendez took the hand she held out to him and raised it to his lips courteously. ''ow are you, Señora Knight?' He managed the English with a wide apologetic grin at them both and Jason added, 'Ramón is only just beginning to tackle our language.'

The conversation continued between the two men in Spanish, and presently Señor Mendez left them, with many smiles and bows towards her. Jason said, 'He's a decent chap and very hospitable. He insists that we spend the night at his house—says our hotel is not good enough for such an elegant lady.' Again the glittering narrowed smile, the enigmatic curve of the mouth. 'He's gone to fetch his wife and she will look after you while I go back to the hotel and collect our things. Then Ramón plans to show us his floor show before we go back to his home for the night.'

'Oh, that will be lovely.' She smiled with relief at the thought that they wouldn't have to go back to that room in the hotel. She didn't believe that Jason had meant to fix up a separate room for her. She believed that he had meant to—to use her, as he'd said. To make her pay. At that point her imagination had panicked. But now it was all right. Now they would be staying with his friend and business associate, whose goodwill obviously meant a great deal. So long as they were in Ramón Mendez's home she was safe.

Señor Mendez returned to their table, bringing his wife, a handsome woman in a fashionable black dress. She wore her hair piled on top and held by a comb, with a tiny red rosebud tucked into it, and she had a wide, friendly smile.

'*Mucho gusto en conocerle*, Señora Knight,' she beamed, holding Sara's hand in hers, and launching into a flood of Spanish, until her husband stopped her, indicating with a smile Sara's baffled expression. After that

Señora Mendez showed her pleasure at meeting Sara with nods and waves of the hand.

When the men had left them she took Sara's arm and led her between the tables to a large, cool patio roofed with bamboo at the back of the restaurant. Here a band was playing in a corner, half hidden by trailing green leaves. Couples were dancing, or sitting around with drinks. More couples were drifting out from the dining room all the time. The women's attire varied from the exotic to the frankly outrageous; the music was Spanish and seductive; there was a lush atmosphere of sensual enjoyment. Everyone was having a wonderful time.

With her new sense of escape from danger, Sara relaxed a little. When Señora Mendez gestured to a waiter and he brought long, cool, delicious drinks for them both she drank hers with pleasure and nodded and smiled and felt as if she were taking part in some crazy play where nobody had explained the plot to her, or what part she was supposed to be playing.

After a time the two men returned and more drinks were brought. The floor show began, the music changed, became strident, the flamenco dancers appeared. Everything began to merge together, pounding at Sara's senses: the heady music, the swirl and stamp of the dancers, the colours, the cries, the crescendo of excitement. When it was over she felt more bemused than ever.

She heard Jason's voice in her ear. 'Come and dance.' He pulled her on to the floor, holding her close against him, trying no fancy steps but moving to the rhythm of the music. It was soothing and delightful. Hardly knowing what she was doing she cuddled closer, resting her head against the soft silk of his shirt, feeling the hard muscular warmth of his body through the thin material, conscious of the steady beat of his heart as if it were a reassurance. His cheek came down on her hair and she closed her eyes, forgetting it was Jason Knight who was holding her, forgetting everything except that she felt peaceful and safe for the first time for days.

His head moved, his cheek slid against hers and she felt the roughness of it and was dreamily aware of the faint scent of some aromatic toilet-water or aftershave she had noticed before. Then he bent his head lower and slowly, deliberately, moved his mouth against hers.

Strange new sensations awoke in Sara, quivering along her nerves, pulsing through her blood. Only half aware of what she was doing, she curled a hand round his neck, drawing his mouth closer, lost in this urgent new awareness of her own body.

Then, suddenly, she realised that the music had stopped and he had released her. As he led her back to their table Señora Mendez was clapping her hands and there was a knowing, indulgent smile on her wide, good-natured face. Sara was suddenly overwhelmed by remorse. She had no idea how much Jason had told their hosts of the circumstances—probably not very much, she guessed—but it was shaming to think that Señora Mendez should have seen what had just happened, so soon after Tim—horror and self-disgust ran through her as she realised that while she had been in Jason's arms, the memory of Tim had disappeared, just as if none of it had ever happened.

The Señora was smiling more broadly now. She said something in Spanish to Jason, and he, smiling back, drew Sara closer as they stood beside the table.

She moved in his arms. 'What did she say?' she whispered imploringly. 'What must she think?'

His mouth had its ironic twist as he looked down at her. 'She said how touching it was to see the newly-married lovebirds together, or words to that effect,' he said. 'It seems there's been a slight misunderstanding.'

The shock was like a plunge into icy water. 'But—but——' she stammered under her breath, speaking in a whisper as if the two sitting at the table could understand every word. 'You must tell them—make them understand——'

'Too complicated!' Jason's words were a drawl. 'You can explain if you like,' he added laconically.

Sara was stone-cold sober now and very angry. All the blissful reassurance of those moments in his arms when she felt safe and protected were wiped out as if they had been a dream.

Ramón Mendez was standing up now. He spoke to Jason and Jason took Sara's arm. 'Come along, *Señora Knight*,' his voice mocked her. 'We're leaving now, and there's nothing you can do about it, is there, except make a stupid ugly scene which won't get you anywhere.'

She stared up at the hard face above her, hating him. It was true, dismally, abysmally true. She was his prisoner here as certainly as if he had clapped handcuffs on her, linking her to him.

But you just wait! Jason Knight, she muttered under her breath as she followed him out to the big car that was waiting outside the restaurant. One of these days you'll be sorry for the way you've treated me. One of these days you'll take back every beastly suspicion you have of me!

That day couldn't come soon enough. But meanwhile, she thought with a cold, sinking feeling inside her, meanwhile she had to live through the night ahead.

# CHAPTER FIVE

THE unreal feeling of taking part in a crazy play went on for Sara. Or perhaps it wasn't a play; it was more like a Hollywood film. Everything was sumptuous and smooth and luxurious, from the huge glossy car that drove them along a wide, tree-lined boulevard, to the Mendezes' house that stood, modern and exquisite, in its lush garden of flowers and trailing shrubs that sent out a subtle perfume into the night air.

Inside, the house fulfilled its outside promise, but by this time Sara had ceased to register details. She sank into a deep, satin-covered sofa, which Señora Mendez indicated with a wave of a plump hand, and waited for what would happen next with a kind of fatalism.

A house steward in a white coat brought coffee on a silver tray and placed it on a glass-topped table before Señora Mendez. She pointed to the tall, ornate coffee pot and looked enquiringly towards Sara. '*Negro? Con crema?*' She said the words slowly, eyebrows raised in encouragement.

Sara glanced towards Jason, who was standing with Señor Mendez at the far end of the long, beautiful room, admiring a painting. She made a guess. 'Oh—*negro, por favor*,' she tried shyly.

Her hostess chuckled with pleasure and passed over black coffee in a beaker decorated with a Mexican motif.

Sara had a small sense of triumph too. She'd got it right, and black coffee would help to keep her head clear. She tried her luck again. '*Muchas gracias, señora.*'

Señora Mendez nodded her dark head so energetically that the little red rose in her hair wobbled. She called something across the room, and the two men strolled back towards them.

Jason lowered his long body into the sofa, close beside Sara. He laid his arm along the cushioned softness behind her head and leaned towards her, smiling his twisty, enigmatic smile. 'Who's the clever girl, then, picking up the language?'

She took a sip of the strong black coffee. 'I hate you,' she said into the rim of the beaker, and heard his soft laugh. She saw Señora Mendez regarding the two of them complacently, nodding, evidently enjoying the teasing, loving antics of the newly-weds.

It was ridiculous, maddening, thought Sara in helpless wrath. Here they were, the four of them : Señor Mendez and his wife on one side and she on the other, with Jason playing pig-in-the-middle and being as evasive and misleading as he chose!

If only there were something she could do! If only she could communicate somehow with Señora Mendez and say she must have a room to herself tonight! But even if she knew the words—which she didn't—she certainly couldn't begin to explain the reason for the request. The bright new gold of her wedding ring blinked back at her mockingly. Oh, it was hopeless! Tiredly she laid her head back against the soft cushion behind it and at the same moment she felt Jason's fingers move to lift her hair, exploring the softness of her neck beneath. She shivered violently, spilling her coffee into the saucer.

He took the beaker out of her hand. 'Too bad— *querida*!' he drawled and, leaning nearer, whispered, '*Querida* means darling, by the way.'

He went over to the table and Señora Mendez fussed

around, pouring coffee into another beaker and sending little glances of concern across at Sara, while she chattered away to Jason.

He brought the beaker back to Sara and settled down beside her again. 'Our hostess thinks you look weary and asks if you'd like to go off to bed. I said I thought it was a very good idea,' he added with exaggerated innocence. 'She'll show you to our room when you've had your coffee. I'll have a final nightcap with Ramón and join you later.'

Without another look at her he stood up and joined Ramón beside a table laden with glittering bottles and glasses.

Sara gulped down her coffee and was appalled to see that her hand was shaking. Señora Mendez swooped across the space between them, her stiff black dress rustling, and took the place that Jason had vacated, placing an arm kindly around Sara's waist and murmuring little words in Spanish that were obviously intended to convey sympathy. Sara found herself being led up a staircase and into a wide room, cool and airy, with windows open on to a balcony. The room was probably furnished as luxuriously as the rest of the house, but the only thing that Sara's eyes focussed upon was the enormous double bed with its creamy satin coverlet, against the far wall.

Señora Mendez was holding her arm, leading her around, sliding back doors, showing her in sign language where everything was, even teaching her a few words. '*El cuarto de baño*'—she opened a sliding door to a private bathroom. '*La toalla, el jabón*'—she held up a towel and soap. Sara made herself enter into the fun, repeating the words after her hostess, although she had never felt less like playing games in her life. And when they returned to the bedroom and Señora Mendez patted the bed and murmured '*La cama – la cama matrimonia*,' with a broad smile, Sara could only gulp, for the words refused to come out.

At last the good lady turned to the door, touching Sara's shoulder lightly with a '*Buenas noches.*' She kissed Sara's cheek and then stood back regarding her, her brown eyes misty. '*Muy guapa*,' she murmured.

Sara smiled back, not understanding but guessing that the words meant something pleasant. '*Muchas gracias*,' she answered, and that seemed to please Señora Mendez very much, for she was still smiling as she went out of the room.

Alone, Sara's eyes travelled round the big room, drawn back inevitably to the bed. *La cama matrimonia*—the marriage bed! But she wasn't married to the man who would be coming to join her at any moment. She hadn't any doubt about what his intentions were, he'd made that quite clear. Every nerve and muscle in her body began to quiver with tension until she was hardly breathing. She went out on to the narrow, wrought-iron balcony and stood staring down. The house was enclosed by its gardens, but through the trees she could see the distant lights of the hotels, star-studded giants against the black velvet sky. Below her, in the garden, there was a glint of water from the swimming pool. It was directly below the balcony, she could just make out the pale glow of the tiled surround. From the direction of the boulevard came the soft hum of passing cars. Her fingers gripped the balcony rail and a mad idea came into her mind that if she climbed over, dropped the ten feet or so into the water which would break her fall, she might be able to get to the road, to stop a passing car, hoping it might belong to an American tourist, to plead for help——

She drew in a quivering breath, put one toe of her

scarlet sandal into a whorl of the wrought iron railing, lifted herself a few inches—

'Thinking of making a bolt for it? enquired Jason's deep voice behind her. 'I shouldn't you know. If you didn't knock yourself out, you'd only end up at the police station, and I should probably have a hell of a job getting you released. Better wait for your dear Ralph to find out where you are and then I've no doubt *he'll* get in touch with you.'

She was breathing with difficulty as his hand closed over her arm, drawing her back into the bedroom. He pushed her down against the silken cushions of the bamboo couch which stood before the window, and threw himself down beside her. She saw that there was a bottle and two glasses on the low table beside the couch. He must have brought them up with him. He poured some of the clear brown liquid into each glass and held one out to her.

'I came prepared,' the strange-cloured eyes held hers. 'It's Moctezuma, one of Mexico's famous beers. Sorry I couldn't manage champagne,' he mocked, 'It should be champagne, shouldn't it? The standard accompaniment to a night of love.'

She shrivelled up into a corner of the couch, as far away from him as she could possibly get, her eyes enormous, her heart thumping against her ribs.

He tossed off his beer, put down his glass and stretched out a hand towards her. She moved away even further, crossing her arms in front of her.

There was a long silence. His gaze moved over her with slow deliberation, and it was as if he had touched every part of her. 'Not playing hard to get, are you?' he said, 'It's rather late in the day for that, surely.'

'I—I don't know what you mean,' she stammered.

His laugh wasn't pleasant, 'Oh, come now, don't pretend you didn't know what you were doing when you made your offer, earlier on. Lying there on the hotel bed, gazing up at me with those big violet eyes of yours. "Jason—couldn't we be friends?" ' He mimicked her voice hatefully. 'Friends! There's only one kind of friendship I'd know about with a girl like you.'

He turned towards her, his hands on her shoulders, pushing her back against the couch. 'You disgusted me at first,' he said, his mouth curling. 'Then, later on, I thought why not? Why the hell not? Why shouldn't I take what I could get from you—it would be a tiny payment for what you've taken from me.' His face loomed above her, dark and disturbing.

Her lips were shaking convulsively. 'I didn't make any offer. I didn't mean—I only wanted us to be friends —*please*, Jason!' She didn't realise she was still holding the glass he had given her until she heard it drop to the floor and felt the cold liquid dripping over her bare legs.

He must have felt it too, for he raised his head and suddenly his mood seemed to change, the mockery came back to his voice. 'You do throw your drinks around, don't you? It must be the unnerving effect of my presence.' He picked up the glass and put it back on the table. 'Have some of mine instead.' He poured some more of the Moctezuma beer into his own glass, drank from it, then leaned across to hold it to her lips. Sara took a sip and it was cool and refreshing to her dry, parched mouth.

He put the glass down. 'My God, girl, you've drenched yourself!' His mouth pulled into a grimace. 'I draw the line at making love in an aroma of beer. Let's have this dress off.' Before she knew what he was going to do he had unzipped the scarlet chiffon and pulled it from her shoulders, easing it quickly down to her hips. 'Up

you get!' Standing before her, he lifted her to her feet
with one quick movement, and the dress fell about her
ankles to the floor.

Sara found it possible to speak at last. 'H–how dare
you? Pushing me about as if I were a—a doll!'

He grinned sardonically. 'Well, you are, aren't you?
Quite a doll!' His eyes roamed appreciatively over her
slim, golden-brown body as she stood before him in her
lacy bra and panties, and she felt the heat throb from
her toes to her cheeks. Desperately she looked round for
escape and saw the door to the bathroom. If she could
gain a little time she might come up with some idea of
how to cope with this situation.

She said, with as much dignity as she could com-
mand, 'I'll go and take a shower, as you object to the
smell of beer.'

Much to her chagrin Jason laughed aloud at that.
'Oh, I don't object to it, but I don't find it much of an
aphrodisiac. And if you're too young and innocent to
know what that means,' he added with heavy sarcasm,
'it means that it doesn't turn me on.'

'Oh!' fumed Sara. She picked up the soaking dress and
slashed at him with it. He made a lunge towards her,
but she was too quick for him and had reached the bathroom before he could touch her.

She closed the sliding door with a thud and stood with
her back to it, breathing quickly, half expecting him to
pull it open from the other side. But nothing happened
and after a minute or two she slid out of bra and panties
and stepped into the wide, jade-green bath, turning on
the taps of the shower until the water ran out pleas-
antly tepid.

Standing under the cascading water she tried to think
what to do, what to say, to make him believe the truth
of the situation. But her mind refused to suggest any

course of action. Jason Knight wasn't prepared even to listen to her, let alone believe her. And he was determined—determined and angry—although his mood had swung from the dark anger that frightened her to a kind of contemptuous amusement. She wasn't sure which was worse.

Thrusting her hand between the curtains of the shower, she leaned over the bath and reached for the scarlet dress, squeezing it out under the water until the smell of the beer had gone. Then she turned off the shower and stepped out on to the curly white carpet, hanging the dress across the bath fitment to drip, and noting that the chiffon seemed to be a washable type of material, as it was hanging crisply. It gave her an odd satisfaction that the dress wouldn't be spoiled, though she couldn't imagine why, as she would never wear it again if she could help it. Jason had presumably brought her clothes from the hotel. There weren't many of them, only the change of undies he had brought to the hospital, and the worse-for-wear white outfit she had travelled in. She would have to wear the white thing again tomorrow, she thought.

*Tomorrow.* She caught sight of her naked body in the mirror that covered one wall of the bathroom and stared back at herself with wide, frightened eyes. What would have happened by tomorrow?

She dried hastily on a fleecy green towel, dusted herself with talc from an elaborate container, and picked up her pants from a stool. With a sinking heart she noticed that they smelled disgustingly of beer. Her bra too.

She stood quite still for all of sixty seconds, holding the offending garments in her hand, feeling hollow inside. Then, making up her mind, she tossed them into the bath, turned on the taps and squeezed them out

as she had done the dress. When this was done she
wrapped herself in the towel closely, pushed back the
sliding door about an inch and applied one eye to the
gap.

Jason had removed shirt and trousers (had they caught
the spilled beer too?) and put on a thin silk dressing
gown in a maroon colour He was lying on the bed, a
picture of relaxed masculinity, with his hands clasped
behind his head, gazing up at the ceiling.

His head turned as he heard the bathroom door slide
back.

'Please,' said Sara in a small voice, 'could you pass me
the rest of my clothes? The ones you brought from the
hotel.'

Lazily he swivelled his long legs off the bed and came
towards her. 'What makes you think you'll be needing
clothes any more tonight?' he enquired with that twisty
smile of his. He stood looking down at her, swathed in
the huge green towel. Then he sniffed. 'Ah, that's better!
Very seductive!'

He moved closer and she retreated into the bathroom,
but he slid the door open with one flick of a strong
arm. The other hooked itself round her neck, pushing
away the fine, damp hair, unerringly finding a sensitive
spot so that she shivered violently again. He smiled and
his fingers moved down her spine. 'Cool,' he murmured.
'Cool and beautiful.' There was a new note in his voice
now, thick and reckless.

'I don't—please let me go——' She tried to pull his
arm away, but it was like steel under her puny strength
and she dropped her hand again in an effort to hold the
towel, which was slipping lower and lower.

She was suddenly overcome by her own inexperience.
She had read books, seen films, of sexual encounter, but
nothing seemed to have prepared her for this situation.

Nothing had prepared her, either, for the way her body was behaving under his touch, as if little flames were licking at it, warming, relaxing, melting away the resistance she knew she should be making.

She drew in a shaky breath. 'Jason, you *must* listen to me. This—what you're asking of me—I can't. You misunderstood what I said. I wouldn't be any good to you,' she added desperately. 'Not what you expect——'

'I know what I expect.' He grasped the green towel and pulled it away from her body. 'You're not going to back out now,' he muttered, 'by God, you're not.'

He scooped her up in his arms and carried her across the room, the green towel dragging on the floor behind them. Then he dropped her down on to the big, soft bed and threw himself down beside her. 'No more talking,' he whispered huskily, and his mouth closed over hers, hard and angry and possessive. One knee lay across her legs, pinning her down as he pressed her closer and closer, moulding her body against his.

Sara was almost lost. Deep ripples of feeling such as she had never known before were coursing through her, the promise of an ecstasy she had never even imagined. Her hands went up behind his head, her fingers probing into the thick, springy hair. Her mouth softened beneath his mouth. Why not? Why not? a voice inside her seemed to be saying as she felt all resistance draining away from her. Perhaps I *do* owe it to him. Perhaps it *was* my fault that Tim——

Tim!

It was as if a firecracker had exploded in her head. Suddenly she was pushing him away, fighting with every bit of her strength.

'No—no—no——' she moaned against his chest. 'Not you. Not like this. It should be Tim. Tim should have been the first——'

With a gasp she stopped fighting. Her head sank back against the pillow and tears streamed down her cheeks.

She was vaguely conscious that Jason's body had gone rigid, as if with shock, and that he had rolled away from her. Blindly she groped for the edge of the silk coverlet and pulled it over herself, turning on one side and drawing up her knees as if she could make herself small and as insignificant as possible, fighting to control the tears that tore at her throat.

When at last she got herself under control, she dared to turn her head. Jason was sitting on the edge of the bed with his back to her, his head buried in his hands. There was something defenceless in the droop of his wide shoulders that touched her unbearably, against all reason. 'I'm sorry,' she heard herself whisper.

Jason didn't turn his head. 'All right, you win,' he said wearily. 'Maybe I'm not such a swine as I thought I was.' He got to his feet, draping the maroon dressing gown round him. 'Cover yourself up and get some sleep,' he said, not looking at her. 'I'm going to take a shower— a very cold shower,' he added grimly. 'And tomorrow we start back to England.'

Without another word or a glance in her direction he walked across to the bathroom and the door slid closed behind him.

Sara lay staring at the door, feeling sick, her emotions in turmoil. Sleep, he had said. She felt as if she would never sleep again. But she had reckoned without the relaxation that follows unbearable tension. Suddenly her whole body went slack and she found herself yawning over and over again. The night had turned cool, but she was too exhausted, even, to look for a nightdress. Burrowing deeper under the bedclothes on one side of the big bed, Sara slept.

*

It was morning and sunshine was seeping between the cream satin curtains that covered the long windows. Sara opened her eyes and was immediately aware of everything, in a lightning-flash of memory. For a long moment she lay absolutely still, holding her breath. Then, stealthily, she moved her head until she could see the other side of the wide bed. It was unoccupied, the cream satin pillow plump and undented.

Very cautiously she drew herself up. The morning air came in cool puffs through the open window, blowing the curtains apart and striking chill against her bare skin. She pulled the covers up to her nose and looked round the room. Except for herself it was empty. Jason's maroon dressing gown was slung over the back of the bamboo couch, his putty-coloured travelling case stood open on a chair and his brushes and electric shaver reposed on the built-in dressing table across the room. The sliding door into the bathroom was ajar and no slightest sound came from within.

The shiny carrier bag that Jason had brought to the hospital with her new clothes was standing beside the closet. She drew in a quick breath, slid out of bed, grabbed the bag and flew across the room into the bathroom, dragging the door to behind her. Once inside she began to breathe more easily again as she took a quick shower and got into the new bra and panties from the bag. The white dress looked rather a wreck; it was fairly obvious that Jason, with masculine indifference, had stuffed it into the bag from where it had hung over the back of the chair in the hotel room. The thought of asking for an iron presented mountainous problems. Sighing, she smoothed the skirt over her hips, pulled the sleeveless top over her head and shook out the little jacket. It would have to do.

She surveyed her face in the mirror, rather surprised

that it showed no sign of last night's stresses. If anything, she looked better, she had to admit; her eyes were clearer and there was a tinge of colour in her cheeks. She pulled a comb through her hair, straining it back from her small oval face in the style Ralph had always insisted on her wearing, saying it gave her a distinguished, 'ballerina' look. Now, remembering that, she felt a quick revulsion and ran her fingers through the pale, silky mass until it lifted and curved and fell over her ears and forward against her cheeks. She tossed her head, making her hair bounce from side to side, and felt a sense of exhilaration. She was free from Ralph—free for good, and she had Tim to thank for that.

Her mouth trembled. Poor darling Tim; she would have made him happy, she would have given him everything he asked if she had been allowed time. But it wasn't to be, she thought very sadly.

She dragged her mind back to the present situation. She was still prisoner while she was in Mexico with Jason, there was no way she could get away from him. No money, no training for a job, hardly a word of the language—it was hopeless. But he had said they were starting back for England today and she had to believe him. There was light and freedom at the end of the tunnel.

Last night—but she wouldn't let herself think about last night. She would pretend it had never happened. For some reason she felt quite sure that she wouldn't have to cope with a situation like that again; sure that Jason would leave her alone in future and not try to exact some kind of revenge. Yes, she would put last night behind her, never give another thought to the effect his lovemaking had had on her. He was a sophisticated man, she told herself, of *course* he was an expert lover. Of *course* he would know exactly how to arouse her. She would simply put it down to experience and the growing-up process, and forget all about it.

Her mind might decide it was a good thing to forget, but her body didn't. Her body remembered vividly the touch of Jason's hands, and the hot awakening passion inside her, thrilling through every nerve. Impatiently she swung away from the mirror. The memory would go, it *had* to. She couldn't let herself fall in love with Jason Knight, it was simply unthinkable.

She heard the door of the bedroom open. His voice called sharply, 'Sara!' and then, after a pause, more urgently, 'Sara, where are you?' The bathroom door slid open and he stood there, almost filling the doorway with his size, looking even larger than ever in his light travelling suit. 'Ah, there you are!' Was it relief that passed over his face? Did he believe she'd managed to escape?

The sudden sight of him had sent shock waves of something that felt like fear in the pit of her stomach, but she pulled herself together quickly.

'Good morning,' she said, and took a step towards the doorway into the bedroom.

He didn't move. The odd, clay-coloured eyes were searching her face and he was frowning slightly. He said, 'You've done your hair differently. It makes you look younger. By the way, how old *are* you?'

'I'm eighteen,' said Sara coolly.

Just for a moment she thought she saw shocked surprise in his face. But she must have been mistaken, for he just shrugged and moved back for her to come out into the bedroom.

The steward who had served coffee last night was coming into the room carrying a large, heavily-laden tray. At a word from Jason he flicked down legs from beneath it, turning it into a table, and set it down in

front of the bamboo couch. He then hovered, brown
face wreathed in amiable smiles, until Jason dismissed
him with a nod and a word of thanks.

'Breakfast,' said Jason briskly, sitting down and patt-
ing the seat beside him. 'We mustn't take too long over
it. Ramon's very civilly offered to get us a flight back
to Mexico City and his private car will take us to the
airport. H'm, this pineapple juice is good.' He tossed it
down appreciatively.

Sara sat down on the couch, leaving as much distance
as she possibly could between them. Last night, she
thought, he would have remarked on that with his
twisted, ironic smile, but this morning he didn't seem
to notice. 'Eggs? Tortillas?' He pushed the dishes towards her and went on with his breakfast, leaving her to
enjoy hers. Which, after a minute or two of wariness,
she did. If Jason were going to adopt this new, casual
attitude towards her, as if she were a younger sister—
someone he was taking along with him but didn't have
to be particularly polite to—it would make things easier
all round. Certainly *she* didn't wish to extend or deepen
their relationship, did she? Resolutely she kept her eyes
turned away from him while she finished her breakfast, and no further word passed between them.

They left the Mendez home very soon afterwards.
Señora Mendez, Sara gathered, had a slight headache
and was still in bed, but her husband was there to say
'*Adiós*' and receive Jason's thanks for his hospitality.
Sara smiled at him and produced, '*Muchas gracias,
señor*,' from her limited repertory, which seemed to
please him mightily, for he kissed her on both cheeks
and made a lengthy and obviously flattering remark
about her to Jason.

He stood waving to them from the steps as the big

car glided away. 'He's nice,' said Sara, warmed by the Mexican's friendliness. 'What did he say?'

Jason regarded her without expression. 'He said you were a very beautiful, kind, gentle, and in every way desirable lady and I was the luckiest man in the world to have such a wife. Does that amuse you?' he added drily.

All Sara's pleasure evaporated. 'I just thought he was nice, that was all,' she said wearily. How he must hate her, she thought, if he managed to turn even the simplest remark into a needle-sharp weapon to use against her.

He turned away disinterestedly as the luxury car moved through the traffic on the boulevard and out on to a bridge across the lagoon—incredibly blue in the morning sun. 'A satisfactory visit,' he mused. 'With luck there should be some very happy results from it.'

He wasn't speaking to Sara, he was talking to himself. And the results he was congratulating himself upon were business matters. But she couldn't help thinking that there already *had* been results for her, and none of them could be remotely considered either lucky or happy. Sitting in her corner she studied the face of the man beside her, lost in his own thoughts. Every part of it, every detail, seemed to be etched in her mind. The dark brown, wiry hair, pushed carelessly to one side; the strange, clay-coloured eyes with the darker rims to the irises; the dominant nose and chin and the long, mobile mouth that could so easily twist into contempt. But for a moment last night his lips had been gentle, brushing against hers, teasing her into sensual arousal. She closed her eyes and a shiver ran through her as she lived that moment again, and as the realisation came to her with the illumination of a lightning flash that she *wanted* to live it again, not just in memory, but in fact. She wanted so desperately to feel herself in his arms again that she almost felt she was falling towards him on the seat of the car.

Horrified, she opened her eyes to find his eyes upon her. The heat surged into her cheeks and she shrank back instinctively, although he hadn't touched her.

He moved his shoulders impatiently. 'Relax, for goodness' sake, Sara! Anyone would think I was a monster of vice, the way you're behaving. You've nothing to fear from me—I don't seduce unwilling women. Last night was unfortunate, but I don't think I could be blamed for believing you'd issued an invitation. I might have known that you'd been well trained by your stepfather. You don't pay your debts either.' His lips curled.

She swallowed convulsively. 'I don't owe you anything.'

His narrowed gaze seemed to shrivel her up. 'That,' he said, 'is a matter of opinion.'

There was a silence as the car sped along the road towards the airport. Sara was thankful that it was a limousine, with a glass partition closing off the driving seat in front. Not that the large, coffee-skinned chauffeur wearing the inevitable Mexican slouch straw hat would understand the conversation, she was sure. But her nerves were so raw that she had the feeling that everyone must know what was happening.

'However,' Jason went on as if he had never stopped, 'as I fully intend to pursue my plan of keeping you under my eye until the situation becomes clearer, we'd better come to a working arrangement so that we can have some sort of understanding.'

'Understanding!' Sara burst out bitterly. 'You haven't even begun to understand anything!'

He ignored that, continuing calmly, 'We shall probably have to spend a day or two in Mexico City before we can fly back to England. If we need to stay a night in a hotel I'll make sure you have a separate room.' He treated her to a searing glance and added, 'I certainly wouldn't want to lay a hand on you again.'

This time Sara bit back the quick retort that came to her lips and sat stiffly silent while he improvised his plan. 'You've got to put up with my company for a day or two longer, whether you like it or not—and I'm sure you don't like it any more than I like yours. We shall behave as if we were—' he tilted his head back consideringly—'as if we were distant relatives who've been thrown together temporarily by some family crisis. They dislike each other intensely but have decided to call a truce for the sake of convenience. In company they will be civil to each other, keeping strictly away from personal matters. When there's nobody else around, the less they say to each other the better.' He lowered his head and looked enquiringly at her, eyebrows lifted sardonically. 'How does that appeal to you as a scenario?'

Sara pressed her lips together tightly, then released them just sufficiently to say. 'It's what I would have expected from you.'

'And what do you expect from me?'

'Precisely nothing,' she said.

He smiled sourly. 'Then we should manage very well. To continue: In Mexico City you can buy what clothes you need. I shall come with you as I don't propose to supply you with any money, of let you out of my sight. If we have to stay overnight in a hotel you shall have a room to yourself, under my supervision, of course. Then when we get back home to Dorset I'll hand you over to my Aunt Vera and we can wait until you esteemed stepfather puts in an appearance.'

'He won't,' said Sara. 'I told you, he doesn't know what's happened, or where I am, or anything.'

'No?' he sneered hatefully. 'Well, we shall see. I shall
be very surprised if he doesn't turn up pretty soon, and
when he does I want to be in a position to find out
exactly what his game is—his and yours. I imagine he'll
be willing to settle for a lump sum if it's big enough. I
don't fancy a legal battle with some shady lawyer,
squeezing my company for every penny of Tim's share
in it.'

Sara sighed deeply. She wasn't going to enter into
some financial argument that she didn't understand. She
didn't want any of Tim's money, and certainly she would
make sure that Ralph didn't get any of it, in the un-
likely event of his turning up in her life again.

She said, 'Your aunt—what does she know about—
about everything?'

'Only the bare facts.'

'What facts?' she insisted, and, heatedly, 'Can't you
see you're putting me in an impossible position? What
have you told her about me? About all these fantastic
suspicions you have about me and my motives?'

He studied her face impassively. 'She knows nothing,
as I said. Just the fact that Tim married you on the day
of the train crash, and that I'm bringing you back with
me.'

She met his eyes and they stared at each other across
the width of the car seat. Behind him, through the car
window the passing scene was a blur of brown and
green; she could only focus on those strange, almost
hypnotic eyes that seemed to see right into her. Why
couldn't they see the truth? she thought, in sudden des-
pair. Oh, why couldn't they?

'And that's all you've told her? Nothing else?'

'Nothing. Her health isn't too good and she's quite
sufficiently upset as it is, without hearing about the
more—sordid details of the affair.' He shrugged. 'She'll

make up her own mind about you and I've no doubt
you can charm her into believing you're a dear, sweet,
innocent young girl if you want to. I don't suppose she'll
see you once the settlement is completed. You'll be up
and away on the trail again, in search of bigger game.'

Sara drew in a tight, controlled breath until she felt
as if her chest would burst. 'I think,' she said, 'that you're
the most detestable person I've ever met.'

'Good!' he said. He lay back in his seat and closed
his eyes and no further word passed between them until
they reached the airport.

## CHAPTER SIX

'OUR train leaves in twenty minutes.' Jason turned away
from the booking office in London's Waterloo Station.
'I'll just have time to phone Aunt Vera and let her know
we're on our way.' He was walking briskly towards the
nearest phone box. 'Wait here, Sara, I'll only be a minute
or two.'

Sara waited obediently beside their luggage. For the
last two and a half days she had followed Jason round
meekly, like a docile little poodle on a lead. Cancún
Island to Mexico City—Mexico City to Miami—Miami
to Heathrow—Heathrow to Waterloo Station. She had
left everything to him, agreed amiably with everything
he suggested, thanked him politely when he kept his
promise about her having a room to herself at the hotels
where they stayed overnight. She had spoken when she
was spoken to, and at other times amused herself with
the magazines he bought her.

Now and then she had caught him looking at her in

a puzzled way, as if he were finding it difficult to believe
that she could keep up what he no doubt believed was an
act for so long, without giving herself away.

But it hadn't been an act. It was all part of a plan.
If Jason could make a scenario, so could she, and she
had been thinking about it through the hours and hours
of sitting on planes or in hotel lounges. The success of
the plan depended on Jason taking her back to Dorset
with him, and as that was what he intended to do in any
case she had decided to make the journey as painless as
possible.

Later on, she told herself—later on, when her life was
her own again and she didn't have to rely upon him
for everything—later on it would be very different. Later
on he was going to get quite a surprise. Sara was looking forward to that.

The rush hour hadn't yet started, but Waterloo was
busy, as always. Sara stayed placidly where she was
while the moving flux of travellers drifted round her.
She wore a trouser suit in a deep coral, one of the things
Jason had bought for her in Mexico City. It made her
look appealingly young and slender and, with her golden
hair curving round her lovely small face, she attracted
glances—sidelong and not so sidelong—from every man
who passed, but she didn't notice. Her glance appeared
to be moving casually over the busy forecourt of the
station, but actually she was watching out of the corner
of her eye the tall figure of the man in the grey suit
who was standing half turned towards her as he held
the receiver to his ear, moving his head a little, now
and then, to make sure she was still there where he had
left her.

He had certainly kept his resolve not to let her get
away from him, from the moment they arrived back in
Mexico City from Cancún. With a little stab that felt

like physical pain Sara found herself recalling for the hundredth time that night.

True to his promise Jason had booked separate rooms at the hotel where they stayed. She remembered the grimness of his face as he had entered her room.

'There's a communicating door between us, as you can see,' he said, walking across to the door of her room and locking it on the inside. 'You can come through my room when we go out.' He slipped the key deliberately into his pocket.

'Very well,' Sara had agreed.

He gave her a suspicious glance. 'You're being very meek all of a sudden. Not thinking of trying something on, I hope?'

She smiled sweetly at him. 'Why should I? Isn't it in my interest to stay with you until I've—how did you put it—until I've collected the loot? I shan't object to walking through your room.' With a new courage that she hadn't known she possessed she added, 'Just so long as that's *all* that's expected of me,' and glanced through the open doorway at the bed in the room beyond.

Just for a moment she had broken through his mask of indifference and she had seen anger flare in the strange, clay-coloured eyes. 'Don't worry,' he said savagely, 'I shan't be tempted to fall into that trap again.'

She had believed him, but still she couldn't sleep that night. She lay awake, watching the lights moving across the ceiling from the ceaseless all-night traffic in the street below the window, while a confusion of thoughts and feelings rioted inside her. Around two in the morning, when she could lie still no longer, she got up and paced around the room, coming back time and time again to the closed door that separated her room from Jason's.

If only she could put things right between them, she thought desperately, so that he didn't look at her with

contempt and anger! She had the strangest certainty that
he wasn't asleep either, that if she were brave enough to
go in to him and *make* him listen while she explained
her own part in the tragic events of the past week, she
could convince him that she was telling the truth.

Her heart beating heavily, she had put a shaking hand
on the door knob.

Then from the other side of the door she heard a faint
sound, the springs of the bed creaking. She had a sudden
vivid picture of him lying there, his dark hair rumpled
against the pillow, his eyes sleepily mocking, the shadow
beginning to show on his chin, the long line of his body
under the covers.

The truth hit her like a blow. To talk to him, to
explain, to argue? Who did she think she was fooling?
What she really wanted was to be in his arms again, to
press close against him, to drown in mindless delight
as his hands moved expertly over the soft warmth of her.

A convulsive shudder ran through her whole body.
When she married Tim she had been a child. Now she
was a woman, wanting one man with a hunger and
desperation that shocked her. She hadn't known it could
be like this, and it was bitter that it had to be Jason
Knight who had taught her.

Sick with misery and self-contempt, she had stumbled
back into bed and pulled the covers over her head.

Next morning she had remembered that middle-of-the-
night frenzy and had told herself she was glad it had
happened. With the new knowledge of herself she
would at least be armed against her own weakness.

Jason had finished his phone call now and was making
his way back towards her, a tall man in a well-fitting
grey suit, walking with a lithe arrogance that made
people move out of his way without his doing anything
to demand it.

A difficult, dangerous man, thought Sara, pleased that she could make this critical assessment of him so coolly now. Not a man to tangle with—or to fall in love with. A rueful little smile touched her mouth, but disappeared immediately as he reached her.

'All fixed up,' he said. 'Vera's arranging for us to be met at Wareham. She doesn't drive herself, and there isn't anyone around to bring my car out, so she's ordering a taxi. Come along, our train's in.'

He picked up their luggage and they made their way along the platform towards the first-class section. 'This one'll do.' He stopped beside an open door and stood aside for her to get in.

Sara looked up at the door hanging open above her and suddenly she remembered with blinding accuracy that other train journey. She went icy cold and the door began to sway from side to side before her eyes. She put out a hand and grasped at Jason's arm to steady herself.

'What's the matter?' he asked.

The impatience in his voice brought her back abruptly from the void. She blinked. 'N–nothing, I just—I think I caught my foot on something.' Helplessly she stared down at the platform and kicked at a cigarette packet lying by her foot.

He shrugged. 'Get in then.'

For an agonising moment she thought, *I can't do it. I can't get into the train*. She was going to make a fool of herself.

Jason was waiting. Impossible to explain how she felt —to speak of that other time—with Tim! With a tremendous effort she pulled herself up and stumbled along the corridor and into the empty compartment that he indicated.

She sank into a corner seat, feeling faint and queasy.

Jason put their luggage on the rack and sat down opposite. He unfolded the copy of the *Financial Times* which
he had bought at the station and began to read, ignoring her completely. She was thankful for that; it would
give her time to pull herself together. The last thing she
wanted to do was to pass out when he was there; she
could imagine the ironical gleam in his eye as he thought
it was just another act she was putting on.

March was a slack time of year for travelling, and
afternoon a slack time of day. When the train started
they were still alone in their compartment. Sara leaned
her head against the head-rest and closed her eyes and
told herself that this awful panicky feeling would pass
away soon. Somewhere she had read that when you feel
faint the best thing to do is to breathe very slowly and
deeply. She began to count the breaths—in—out—in—
out——But it just made her feel dizzier than ever.

She opened her eyes and saw the outskirts of London
passing by the window. Just the same way the outskirts
of Mexico City had passed by on that other day. Just
the same way the train had begun to gain speed, the
wheels hissing over the rails, metal against metal. With
a sudden swoosh they met another train and for a few
moments the view was blotted out by lines of carriages
flicking past in the opposite direction, and the clatter
was deafening. They were clear again now, gaining speed
quickly. Sara began to feel deathly cold and the hairs on
the back of her neck were prickling. Her palms were wet
where the fingernails were digging in and there was the
taste of blood in her mouth.

Jason put down his paper and glanced across in her
direction. 'Would you like a cup of tea?' he said. 'I'll
see if there's any going.' He started to get to his feet.
Just as Tim had done, that other time——

Sara's eyes dilated as wave upon wave of sick terror

ran through her body. 'Jason, don't go—don't leave me——'

She wasn't aware that she had thrown herself against him, forcing him back into his seat. She didn't see the amazed look that crossed his face, to be followed by another, totally different expression. She was only dimly aware that she was clinging to him wildly and that his arms were round her, holding her shaking body against his, stroking her hair, comforting her as if she had been eight instead of eighteen.

'All right, Sara—all right, girl—you're safe now. I've got you safe.' The voice was deep and gruff, not like Jason's casual, indifferent way of speaking to her at all.

At last the shaking stopped and she felt limp and drained. Her face was buried against his shoulder; she could feel the strong warmth of him through the stuff of his jacket, smell the now-familiar toilet preparation he used. It was heaven to be held close to him, to feel safe. Coming home must be like this, if you'd ever had a home to come back to.

She didn't move, and he seemed in no hurry to let her go. The train was bucketing along now, out in the country, fields and trees rushing past. But she wasn't afraid any more. She wanted to stay here in his arms, hearing the strong beat of his heart, conscious that her own heart was beginning to steady its wild fluttering and match the rhythm of his, longing to lift her head to see if there was any tenderness in his face. But she mustn't. He might read the truth in her eyes—that she was longing for his kiss.

With an effort she drew away and slid back into her own seat, pushing her hair off her face.

'I'm—I'm terribly sorry,' she stammered. 'That was idiotic of me. You must have thought I was—was——'

'Issuing another invitation?' he said dryly. 'No, not

this time. I can recognise fear when I see it. You were scared stiff, weren't you?'

She nodded dumbly.

'It was because of coming on a train?'

She nodded again. That was part of the truth.

'Not surprising,' he said almost casually. He was looking at her mouth. 'You've got blood on your lip. Here, let me.' He took a folded white handkerchief from his pocket and, leaning towards her, wiped her mouth firmly.

'Thank you,' she said shakily. 'And—and I'm afraid I've bled all over you too.'

He glanced down at his light jacket where her head had rested and flicked the handkerchief carelessly against the small red stain there. 'It'll clean, I expect,' he said carelessly. 'Feeling better now?'

'Oh yes, thank you, much better.' Much, much better. Because he had shown that he could be sensitive and understanding, that he wasn't hard and tough all through. A tiny glimmer of hope rose in her that one day she might be able to make him listen to her and believe her.

'Good,' he said. 'How about finding that cup of tea, then? We'll go together if you don't want to be left alone,' he added matter-of-factly, sliding the door of the compartment open for her to pass through. As she went she turned and said, 'You were kind, Jason. Thank you.'

He shrugged and the ironic gleam was back in his eyes again. 'I wouldn't want to arrive home with a hysterical female on my hands, would I?' he said coolly.

She went out into the swaying corridor before him, disappointment hitting her like a blow. Nothing had changed and she had been a fool to imagine, for a moment, that it might have done.

When they returned from the buffet car the journey

continued without further incident. Jason took out his paper again and Sara flicked through the magazines he had bought for her at Waterloo. Once he lowered his paper and glanced over at her, raising his eyebrows. 'All right now?' he enquired, unsmiling.

'Yes, thank you.' She kept her voice as cool as his.

After a while she closed her eyes and fell into a half-sleep, waking briefly to see the docks and cranes when they stopped at Southampton and then drifting away again.

At the next stop she wakened completely. 'Bournemouth,' she said with a ring of pleasure. 'Oh, we're nearly there.'

Jason looked up from his paper. 'You know this part of the world?'

'Oh yes, I used to go to school here.' Her eyes had a shine in them. It was wonderful to be on familiar ground again after the nightmare of the last days.

'Really?' he said politely, and began to read again.

She winced inside at the snub. But of course she wouldn't expect him to be interested in anything that concerned her, would she? She felt treacherous tears sting behind her eyes as she thought that if it had been Tim sitting opposite, bringing her back to his home as he had planned, he would have asked her questions about the school. They would have laughed together about some of the foolish little incidents she could have made amusing: the awful time she was put in the hockey team because everyone who could really play had 'flu and the school lost by ten goals to nil; the cookery exam when she forgot the baking powder in the scones and they turned into chapattis; the pantomime when she played the fairy queen and made quite a hit.

She blinked back the tears. Tim wasn't here and there was nobody to share things with. Jason hated her and his aunt would most probably feel as he did about her share in the tragedy. She ached with loneliness.

Very soon the train drew into Wareham station and Sara walked beside Jason down the platform. They were almost the first of the passengers to alight and as they passed through the booking hall and out into the fore-court a tall girl in black trousers and a swingy mink coat slid from behind the driving seat of a stylish red coupé and ran towards them.

'Jason—Jason Knight! But this is extraordinary! I was thinking about you at just that very moment. I'm meeting Oliver—have you seen him on the train?'

Her eyes were blue and round, shining like glass marbles as they fixed themselves on Jason. Then, as if at some inner signal, they softened and the surprised delight changed to a soft, vibrant sympathy. She put both hands on his forearms and kissed him. 'Oh, poor, poor Jason, I'm so terribly sorry about Tim. What a truly awful thing to happen! I simply couldn't believe it when Oliver rang your yard yesterday to see how his boat was getting on, and they told him about the accident. I couldn't sleep last night, thinking of you going through all that, so far away. And all alone too!'

Bright blue eyes rested curiously on Sara, who had stopped beside Jason.

He said, 'Thanks, Diana. But I wasn't alone. I had Tim's wife to look after. Sara, meet Diana Forbes, Diana, this is Sara. She and Tim were married in Mexico, a week ago.'

The full red mouth gaped open as Diana stared, for a moment at a loss for words. 'Oh!' she said. 'I didn't know.' And then, rather woodenly, 'How dreadful for you, my dear!'

Sara murmured something and stood aside a little. These last days, when she and Jason had spent every

waking moment together, she had somehow failed to
realise that he had a life in England, a life with family,
friends, his work. A life in which she herself had no part
at all, except that he wanted to remove her from it as
quickly as possible.

The man called Oliver was last off the train. Jason
would have moved away, but Diana put her hand on
his arm, stopping him. 'Do wait and have a word with
Oliver.' She ran over to a large, fair man who was just
then surrendering his ticket, and spoke rapidly to him.

'This is a nuisance,' said Jason to Sara, in a low voice,
as the other two approached. There were greetings,
introductions, condolences. Sara wasn't taking much of
it in. She felt thankful when the group seemed to be
about to split up. Diana was saying to Jason, 'You must
come and see us very soon, when things have straightened out for you. Come and have dinner.' The blue eyes,
lifted to his, were limpid.

Sara felt her hand grasped once again by the large,
fair man. 'Do come,' he said. 'My sister and I will be delighted to show you our new house. We must take you
out of yourself,' he added with a clumsy attempt at
sympathy which Sara found rather endearing. He was,
she thought, a much more genuine and likeable person
than his sister.

Goodbyes were said. Oliver and Diana got into the red
coupé and set it snorting out of the station. Jason located
the taxi that had been ordered to meet them. 'Come
on,' he said wearily, 'for God's sake let's get home.'

He was silent as the taxi drove them through the
busy little town and out into the country, across the
heath and over the hills towards the sea. Sara, after
one look at his set face, kept silent too. With a pang of
compassion she knew how he must be feeling—coming
home with only her beside him, as a constant reminder

of what he had lost: a brother, a partner, a companion.

She looked at the strong brown hand lying on the seat and longed to stretch out and touch it, to offer comfort as he had so surprisingly comforted her on the train. How impossible! She was the last person in the world he would ever turn to for comfort. In Mexico, when his shock and grief were new, he would have taken her as a drug—an opiate, he had called it. But now he was back in his own home, among his own people, his own friends, and he didn't need her even as a drug.

She remembered the way Diana Forbes had lit up when she saw him, the way she had kissed him, gazed softly at him. There was no mistaking the message in those acquisitive, round blue eyes. Was she someone very special in his life? She winced away from the thought, telling herself that it was because she had disliked Diana from that first moment. But something that lay deeper in her mind knew that wasn't true. The fact was that the thought of Diana Forbes—or any other girl—in Jason's arms was a poison that could eat into her and destroy her if she wasn't careful. She must take herself out of Jason Knight's life and start to make a new life for herself as soon as she possibly could.

She drew further into her corner and stared out of the window, and as the ragged ruins of ancient Corfe Castle came into sight, bleak against the grey March sky, they seemed a fitting background to her mood.

Soon after that the car slid down a hill, passed through a tiny village, climbed part-way up another hill that was more a track than a road, then turned in between two tall pillars and pulled up before a grey stone house. As she got out of the car Sara could see round the side of the house, across a stretch of grass, to where the land fell away, and beyond that a wide stretch of slate-coloured sea, sullen under low clouds and flecked with tossing white-topped waves. She had a moment of sheer, unthinking pleasure—of homecoming, for Dorset was the only home she remembered and this was Dorset at its best, with the hills behind and the sea in front of her.

Jason paid the driver and the taxi disappeared down the lane. He turned to Sara. 'Welcome home—Mrs Knight,' he said with his ironic smile, and all her pleasure evaporated as she followed him into the house.

Aunt Vera was a surprise. Sara had vaguely expected someone tall and dark and faintly forbidding, a kind of older, feminine counterpart of Jason, but the woman who came across the tiled hall to meet them was of medium height with light brown hair curling over a neat head, and a mouth that looked as if it would smile easily.

It wasn't smiling now. She kissed Jason and held him close for a moment in a silent expression of sympathy. Then she turned to Sara and, without waiting for any introduction, held out her arms to her, too, and hugged her close. It said more than any words could have done, and Sara felt suddenly weak with relief. She had expected hate, or at any rate suspicion, for she hadn't altogether believed Jason when he had told her that Aunt Vera knew nothing but the 'bare facts'. But evidently he had been telling the truth.

The older woman held her away at last and looked over her shoulder at Jason. 'You didn't tell me,' she said.

'Tell you what?' He had moved across the room and picked up the top letter from a stack of unopened ones on the big mahogany desk in the window.

'That Sara was such a darling.' Her voice was warm.

The ironic glance swept over Sara. 'Didn't I?' he said. 'I must have forgotten.' His face had its most enigmatic look as he turned away and slit open the envelope with an ivory letter-opener.

His aunt looked sharply from him to Sara, then her face softened. 'You must be absolutely fagged out, my dear, after all that travelling. I've got tea ready, and we'll have a proper meal later on. Now, you sit down and I'll go and brew up.'

Sara glanced towards Jason, who had his back to them, reading his letter. She shrank from being left alone with him. 'Couldn't I come with you?' She didn't realise that her voice was pleading. 'I seem to have been sitting down for ages and ages.'

Vera Knight had seen the direction of her glance. She raised her eyebrows a fraction. 'Of course you can,' she said, and added with firmness, her eyes on the man by the window, 'This is your home now, my dear, you must do just as you like.'

In the airy, comfortable kitchen she filled a kettle and switched it on. Waiting for it to boil she leaned back against the sink unit and surveyed Sara, standing pale and huddled in her pretty coral trouser suit.

She said, 'Sara, my dear, I've been trying to think all day what I should say to you. This is such a strange, difficult, tragic situation. But now I've seen you, everything I thought of seems too formal, because I feel we're going to be friends. I hope you do too.'

'Oh, yes.' Sara felt as if a little fire had been lit in an icy room she had been inhabiting all the time she had been with Jason. Then her mouth drooped. 'There's just one thing——'

'Yes?'

Sara gulped. It was difficult, but it had to be said. 'Would you mind if I asked you what Jason has told you—about me, and my marrying Tim, and—and everything?'

The kettle boiled and Vera poured the steaming water

into a large brown family teapot. Then she looked up
and met Sara's eyes with a frankness that couldn't be
questioned. 'Nothing at all, really. He simply said that
you hadn't any family of your own to go to and he was
bringing you back here.'

'Oh!' said Sara hesitantly. Then she blurted out,
'Jason doesn't like me. He blames me for what happened
to Tim.'

Vera put the teapot on a loaded trolley and covered it
with a hand-embroidered cosy. 'Does he indeed? Well,
he'll get over it. Jason can be as unreasonable as most
men and even when he was a small boy he was as stub-
born as a young mule. But I never knew him to sulk
for long, and he was always willing to admit when he'd
made a mistake.'

She paused and her grey eyes were suddenly bleak.
'This awful thing has hit us very hard—all of us—and
it's hit Jason doubly hard because of the firm and all his
plans for it. But it isn't anything to do with blame, or
guilt, and we mustn't let ourselves be submerged. Life
goes on and we must go on with it because that's all
we can do.'

She patted Sara's shoulder. 'And you must let me look
after you for a while, my dear, because you look like
a tired little kitten. You need rest and fresh air and
good food, and in a month from now you won't know
yourself.'

A month from now! She couldn't possibly last out
that long, seeing Jason every day, knowing how he hated
her. She must put her plan into action soon. She tried
to think about it as she lay in bed that night in the
warm cosy room that looked out over the sea, with the
moon sailing in and out of scudding clouds, and the
wind howling round the house. Perhaps she *would* stay

here, with Jason's kind and sympathetic aunt, just for a little while. She snuggled down in the soft bed and, for the first time for days, fell asleep immediately.

For nearly three weeks Sara allowed herself to be cosseted. She hadn't meant to stay so long, but she was more exhausted physically than she had known, and each morning, when the daily help came in smiling broadly to plump a healthy-looking breakfast tray on the bed, she found herself revelling in the sheer bliss of doing just what she felt like, with no pressures on her to dress as Ralph wanted her to, always to be at his beck and call to meet his smart, rich friends.

Vera took her into Bournemouth one day, in the bus, and fitted her out with what she called 'seaside kit', which meant navy pants with white rollneck sweaters and a bright blue windcheater. Warm socks and good substantial shoes with thick, springy soles completed the outfit. Clad thus suitably, Sara spent most of the gusty days out of doors, sometimes walking along the edge of the waves on the beach below the house, sometimes climbing up the lane to the top of the headland that reached out into the sea, and standing there with the wind blowing her hair off her face, until she felt somehow cleansed and with a sense of purpose and strength flowing back into her.

She encountered Jason so seldom that she could almost ignore the way her heart thumped when he came into a room unexpectedly, or she happened to meet him briefly on his way to the boatyard in Poole, or coming back from it. He spent all his days there; he was away long before Sara came down in the morning, and often didn't return until she and Vera had finished their evening meal. Then he would eat alone in the dining room and, with a brief glance into the sitting room—out of politeness for his aunt, Sara felt—would disappear into his study and be seen no more that day.

'You mustn't think he's taking himself out of the way because you're here, Sara,' Vera Knight said one evening when this had just happened. She threaded a crewel needle with blue wool and glanced at Sara's faintly troubled face. 'He really has got a great deal on his plate just now, with the boat business. I don't know all the ins and outs, but I know he's been sinking a lot of time and money in this new venture of exporting. Then, of course, they've been working all out at the yard to complete a special order on time—a cruising yacht for a very rich young man who's recently come to live in the neighbourhood.'

'Would it be Oliver something?' Sara enquired.

'That's right, Oliver Forbes. Have you met him?'

'He was on our train, coming from London.' Her cheeks felt warm as she remembered vividly that train journey. 'His sister met him at Wareham.'

'Ah yes, the acquisitive Diana!' Vera Knight plunged her needle into the canvas and added irritably, almost to herself, 'Men can be so utterly blind and stupid sometimes.'

She didn't enlarge on that statement and Sara made no comment. A tight lump seemed to have lodged in her throat and she couldn't have spoken then anyway.

So she hadn't imagined that look in Diana Forbes's blue eyes when they rested on Jason! His aunt knew all about it too. Sara sat staring into the fire in the cosy sitting room of the old grey house that she had grown to love in the last few weeks. She wondered bleakly whether Diana would get Jason in the end and come to live here. One thing she was sure about—she didn't intend to stay to find out. It was time to put her plan into action. Tomorrow.

'Yes, I think a secretarial course will be the best thing for you, Sara. I've no doubt it can be fixed up for you to attend the College.' Miss Glyn, headmistress of Chetwynd School for Girls, stood up, intimating that the interview was at an end.

Sara stood up too and followed her to the door of the study. 'Thank you, Miss Glyn.'

'Of course, if you'd stayed on and taken your A-levels there would have been much more choice.' The inevitable disapproval of girls who let the school down by leaving early was in the headmistress's voice and Sara felt chilled. She had come here intending to confide in Miss Glyn—to tell her the whole story—but when it had come to the point it had been obvious that the headmistress was far too busy to sit and listen to confidences, so all that Sara had said in the end was that she had decided to break away from her stepfather and find some way of supporting herself. She was staying with friends at present, she said, but needed to be independent.

'Yes, Miss Glyn,' she said, feeling a twinge of the awe with which that lady was regarded by every girl in the school. 'It was all a bad mistake.'

Miss Glyn opened the study door. 'I thought it was at the time. But we mustn't dwell on our mistakes, must we? Only learn from them.' Her eyes lingered for a moment on the wide violet eyes in the small sensitive face in front of her and she added more gently, 'Don't worry, Sara. I have your address. I will see what I can do about arranging a course for you and let you know and then, perhaps, you'll come and see me again when I'm not quite so rushed.'

'Yes, Miss Glyn, and thank you very much.' Sara turned to leave, but the headmistress called her back. 'Just one point, Sara. You do realise, don't you, that you need not feel indebted to your stepfather? Your fees here were paid by an insurance company; the policy was taken out by your own father on your birth. Did you know that?'

Sara shook her head. 'No, I didn't. Thank you for telling me, Miss Glyn.'

As she walked slowly down the long drive and waited for the bus to take her back into Bournemouth she felt warmed a little by the thought of the father she had never known, the father who had wanted to do his best for her, and for some obscure reason she felt a little less alone.

But when she got back to Bournemouth and stood on the sea-front, looking out across the water towards the Isle of Wight, the loneliness struck again. She should be feeling pleased with herself for having taken the first step towards a new future, away from Jason Knight, but her interview with Miss Glyn had done nothing to raise her spirits.

She leaned on the promenade railings, a slight figure in her coral trouser suit, and let the breeze blow her hair. In a few weeks the beach and the pier would be teeming with summer visitors, but now, in April, there were only the residents enjoying the spring sunshine. She tried to cheer herself up with the prospect of a secretarial course, but failed. She tried to rally herself; she was young, she had her health, she would make a new life for herself somehow—an exciting life. She would meet another man—lots of other men.

Misery settled over Sara like a dark cloud.

'Hullo, what are you doing here?' said a man's voice behind her.

She swung round, her heart lurching at Jason's voice, colour flooding into her cheeks, life into her nerves and blood and every single part of her.

She said breathlessly, 'I'm not running away, if that's what you were thinking.'

He stood looking down at her and to her surprise he grinned suddenly. 'Well, hardly. You wouldn't get very far on the amount of pocket money you've got.'

She felt ridiculously elated for no very good reason, except that he was there and he wasn't looking angry or contemptuous. 'No,' she said wryly, 'you weren't exactly generous, were you?' When she first arrived she had found an envelope pushed under her door marked 'Petty Cash' in Jason's black scrawl. Inside was a five-pound note.

'I wasn't taking any chances.' He leaned on the railings beside her, tall and hefty-looking in blue slacks and an Aran sweater, his dark hair ruffled by the wind. He said, 'You haven't told me what you're doing in Bournemouth.'

'N–nothing particularly,' she stammered. His closeness was having a very unsettling effect on her. 'I came in with your aunt. She's gone to her embroidery class and I thought I'd have a look round the shops and then take myself back on the bus.'

'No need,' he said. 'I'm going home myself soon, you can come along with me. I've got to call back at the yard first, though. Come along, my car's just back there.'

Sitting beside Jason in the big, powerful car as it wove its way through the streets of Bournemouth in the direction of Poole, Sara tried to think of something to say. It was odd that she should find the silence embarrassing because when she had been alone with Jason before they were either quarrelling or preserving a glacial silence— except for the time on the train from Waterloo, and she preferred not to think about that now. She was so close to him that she could touch the faintly hairy off-white of his sweater if she moved her hand a fraction. Instead she kept her hands tightly clasped together on her lap.

She said nervously, 'It was lucky that you recognised me, standing there.'

'Lucky for you, or for me?' He kept his eyes on the busy road, but she saw a faint smile twitch at the corners of his mouth.

'For me, of course. I shan't have to use my petty cash to pay for the bus now.'

'Ah!' The smile widened slightly. 'Of course.'

Silence fell between them again.

Sara swallowed. 'Is it very big—your boatbuilding yard?'

'Not big enough.' He slowed the car, looking to the right as they approached a big roundabout. 'I was making plans to extend, but——' He left the sentence hanging as the car entered the roundabout and when it was negotiated he made no attempt to finish what he had started to say.

She gave up the attempt to make conversation and sat in silence until the car drew up in front of a large, low building in a back street. Sara hadn't imagined what a boatbuilding yard would look like, but this surprised her as Jason pushed back a heavy sliding door and led the way inside. He had said it wasn't big enough, but it seemed to her vast.

There were perhaps ten or more men at work in different parts of the building. There were what she took to be boats in various stages of construction—some looking like boats already, some more like shells of boats. There was a strong smell of some kind of resin, and the sound of voices echoed hollowly over the whirr of electric equipment.

To the left of them as they went in was a large boat that looked almost finished, except perhaps for the mast and sails. 'Oh, how beautiful!' Sara exclaimed, going over to admire the curving lines of the glossy, pale blue hull with its white bands. The name *DIANA* gleamed whitely on the stern.

She said, 'That's the boat you're building for Oliver Forbes?' and when he nodded, 'It's super, isn't it?' she added admiringly.

'A rich man's toy,' he said. 'I expect you've encountered plenty like her.'

It was true. In her year with Ralph she had sailed with his well-heeled acquaintances on their yachts more than once, but she didn't want to go into that now.

She looked around the whole of the busy building with its stacks of materials, its clean, well-kept appearance. 'It's a huge place.'

'Larger than you expected?'

'I didn't expect anything. I never really thought about it.'

He watched her narrowly. 'No? Well, if you didn't, no doubt there were others who did.'

Anger boiled up inside her and her eyes flashed. She hadn't felt so furious with him since that first day in Acapulco, when he had offered her a cheque. It would serve him right if she smacked his face here, in front of all his workmen. 'Can't you *leave* it?' she hissed. 'I'm getting utterly tired of your suspicions and your innuendoes. You can't still believe it was a confidence trick—that I married Tim for money?'

He rubbed lightly on the hull of the pale blue boat and examined his fingers. 'If it was, you haven't benefited much, to date,' he said mildly. 'We can't put off the reckoning much longer, can we?'

'Reckoning? I don't know what you mean.' There were tears of frustration in her eyes. 'I never know what you mean when you start talking like this.'

His eyes searched her face slowly, moving over every part of it, lingering on her mouth and coming back to meet her own eyes. 'You almost convince me,' he drawled, and to her horror she felt the heat flood into her cheeks.

Then he swung round as a voice hailed him from behind. Oliver Forbes was approaching. He wore an expensive-looking suede jacket and was grinning all over his wide, amiable face. 'Hullo, you two. This is a jolly nice surprise——' as his eyes rested approvingly on Sara. 'How are you, Sara?'

She murmured that she was very well, thank you, and he continued to gaze at her until she began to feel embarrassed and looked away.

Jason said in a businesslike voice, 'Your job's finished on time, Oliver. We'll have her in her berth tomorrow.'

'Oh, good show!' A delighted grin broke over the large face. 'Let's have a celebration. We'll ferry her over to France and——'

Jason broke in. 'Whoa there! Not so fast, my friend. She's got to be put through her paces before we finally hand over, and there's quite a bit of paper work still to do.'

'Gosh!' Oliver was as disappointed as a child denied a treat. 'But we could go aboard once she's afloat?'

'Well, I suppose so,' Jason admitted.

'That's splendid, then.' Oliver was happy again. 'We'll all meet here about half six, shall we? How does that sound? Diana'll be chuffed to death.' He looked towards Sara. 'Put something warm on, Sara. You look pretty gorgeous in that thing you're wearing.' He seemed to be drinking in the sight of Sara in her coral trouser suit. Absently he asked, 'That O.K. with you, Jason? Half six?'

Sara glanced at Jason's face, which was expressionless. 'O.K.,' he said briefly. For a man who has just sold a boat for what must be a five-figure sum he seemed strangely unenthusiastic, she thought.

One of the workmen came up and spoke to Jason, who listened, then raised a hand to Oliver. 'See you,' he said, and went off with the man.

Left alone with Sara, Oliver seemed in no hurry to leave. He stroked the beautiful glossy pale-blue hull of the new boat lovingly. 'I can't wait to see her in the water,' he burst out with schoolboy enthusiasm. 'Diana will be thrilled too. She and Jason have had their heads together over the inside fittings right from the start.' He chuckled knowingly. 'Over more than the fittings, I'd say.' He looked meaningly towards Jason, consulting with two men across the floor. Sara followed his glance, watching the quick, assured movements of the dark head, the litheness of the long, blue-clad legs as he moved from one part of the work on hand to another, listening, speaking, gesturing with that almost arrogant sweep of his arm.

She heard herself say in a muffled voice, 'Is Jason engaged to your sister, then?'

Oliver chuckled again. 'Not officially yet. Maybe tomorrow will be a double celebration.' He lingered. 'I suppose I couldn't buy you a drink or a coffee or something?'

She refused politely and he took himself off with obvious reluctance. She watched him go with a sick, sinking feeling inside. There was no doubt in her mind what the other half of the celebration would most probably be.

# CHAPTER SEVEN

On the way home in the car Jason seemed even more silent than he had been earlier on, but finally he said gruffly, 'Do you really want to go to this do tomorrow, Sara? I could probably get out of it.'

She didn't hesitate. It was going to be agony, but she had to see him with Diana Forbes; after that she could be sure about a lot of things.

'I think it might be fun, she said lightly. She slid a glance towards the chiselled profile of the man beside her. 'Oliver was so keen, and so terribly proud of his beautiful new boat. He's nice, isn't he?' she added thoughtfully.

Just at that particular moment they happened to be crossing the Sandbanks car ferry, wedged in the midst of a wad of cars and lorries and buses, so Jason had time to sit back and give her a long, speculative look. 'Very nice,' he said, with the ironic twist of his lips. 'And *very* rich!'

She couldn't take it from him any longer. 'What's that supposed to mean?' she shot out at him. 'You're sniping at me again. It's a nasty, crabby habit, and I wish you'd stop!'

He lifted dark eyebrows, blinking as if a pet kitten had suddenly spat at him and delivered a painful scratch. 'Yes,' he said thoughtfully, 'maybe it *is* getting a habit.'

By that time the ferry had reached the opposite bank and anything else he might have said was drowned by the noise of engines all firing at once.

Aunt Vera was quite excited about the party. 'What

will you wear, dear?' she asked Sara, at supper. 'It will be chilly on a boat at this time of year.'

Sara nodded. 'Yes, that's what Oliver said. He suggested I should wear the trouser suit I had on this afternoon.'

'Good idea, that was very thoughtful of him and you looked delightful in that pretty coral colour. Doesn't she, Jason?'

On the opposite side of the table Jason cut the final segment from an apple with an incisive stroke. 'Delightful,' he agreed, without looking up.

Aunt Vera continued undeterred. 'You *will* look after Sara, won't you, Jason, and see she doesn't get cold? She's so much better and we don't want her catching a chill and getting run down again.'

He looked up then, with a sardonic smile in Sara's direction. 'I'm sure Oliver will look after her beautifully,' he said, crunching the piece of apple between strong teeth. 'Sara seems to have made a conquest there already. Now, will you excuse me if I leave you? I've got a lot of work to get through.' He picked up his cup of coffee and went out of the room.

His aunt looked after him. 'Well, well!' she said slowly, to nobody in particular, and added with a twinkle, 'Poor Diana!'

Sara almost laughed aloud. Aunt Vera must think there was some tender feeling developing between Jason and herself, and that his display of churlishness was due to jealousy. She could hardly have been further from the truth.

She glanced at the woman beside her, thinking how different Vera Knight had been from what she had expected. Younger too, with her soft curly brown hair and kind eyes, so like Tim's, that could dance with amusement. Young enough and kind enough to understand a great deal that Sara hadn't told her. She said impulsively, 'You've been so good to me since I came here, Aunt Vera. You've just accepted me and haven't asked any questions.'

Vera Knight said placidly, 'When you want to tell me, or to talk about anything, just let me know. It hasn't been the time yet, has it?'

'It will be soon,' said Sara. Before she left finally she would tell Aunt Vera the whole story; she owed it to her. And that would be soon. Much too soon.

Next day the sun shone gloriously and the breeze was warm, more like June than mid-April. The daily woman didn't turn up and Sara insisted on helping in the house, in spite of Aunt Vera's warning that she wasn't strong enough yet for housework.

'I'll dust the bedrooms,' Sara offered. 'That won't hurt me.'

It did hurt, though, when she went into Jason's room. She rubbed and polished vigorously, as if it could ease the hurt, but everywhere she turned he was there. She saw him bending his long back to the dressing table mirror; brushing his hair, dabbing aftershave on his chin; standing at the window looking out over the sea while he thought of his work, the boats he would build, perhaps of Diana Forbes. Not of her—Sara—certainly not of her. If she entered his thoughts at all he would brush her away contemptuously. The certainty of that bit into her like strong acid. Being in love was just slow torture.

She went across the room and smoothed the brown check bed-cover, and her hands lingered sensuously as she felt this new pricking of desire inside herself. Shocked and shaking, she turned and ran out of the room.

The day dragged. After lunch, while Aunt Vera rested,

Sara walked up to the headland and along the cliff path, her feet sinking into the soft turf, her eyes drinking in the wide expanse of sea below, glittering dark blue in the sunlight. Gulls wheeled and screeched as they dived for fish. Once a hare appeared in front of her, front paws lifted, and they regarded each other solemnly before he disappeared like lightning into the bushes. She laughed and wished she could stay for ever in this place she loved.

Jason hadn't put in an appearance all day. He burst in like a cyclone at six o'clock, took the stairs two at a time, and was down again in ten minutes, dark hair wet and gleaming after his shower. In a grey suit with striped shirt and burgundy red tie he looked so devastatingly handsome that Sara's heart turned over at the sight of him.

'You ready?' He hardly glanced at her.

He bundled her into the car, calling goodbye to Aunt Vera in the kitchen, and drove like the wind along the coast road. They just missed the ferry at Sandbanks and had to wait for the next one. When they finally arrived at the boatyard Diana and Oliver were there already.

Jason's car drew up behind the Forbes' red coupé. Diana jumped out and threw her arms round Jason, the moment he got out of his car. 'Isn't this *exciting*?' I was absolutely thrilled when Oliver told me about the party. Oh, Jason darling, you're so *clever* to get our lovely boat finished on time. I've been down just to have a peep from the distance, but I simply can't wait to get on board!' She bubbled over with vivacity.

Sara sat in the car and watched. Diana was a big girl, good-looking in a florid way, with the glow of perfect health. She wore tight navy trousers that fitted her ample legs without a crease, a white furry jacket that hugged her waist, and a saucy nautical cap at an angle

on her dark-gold hair. Sara thought with a sinking heart
that maybe she was the kind of girl that Jason would
marry. All that vigour and fitness—she would be the
right mate for an open-air man who built boats.

'Let's go—I can't wait,' she urged now, tugging at
his arm, taking no notice of Sara, sitting beside them in
the car.

He grinned at her, flicking the hair beneath the blue,
tilted cap. 'Very snazzy!' he teased. 'All ready for the
round-the-world race?'

'Oh, Jay, what a lovely thought—will you come with
me?' The round blue eyes lifted meltingly to his.

He sighed noisily. 'Becalmed in a tropic sea with a
beautiful siren on board! What more could a man ask
for?'

Diana wiggled her hips provocatively and snuggled
against him. 'Heaven! No one's ever called me a siren
before.' Her red lips were parted, only inches below his.

Sara couldn't take any more. They were fooling, of
course, but it was intimate fooling, they knew each other
very well indeed. She slid out of her seat as Oliver
ambled up, saying, 'Hey, you two, break it up! You'll
be having an audience soon.' He looked up and down the
quiet back street. The offices and small stores were closed
and locked, and some children, playing with a ball, were
the only human beings in sight.

Oliver gripped both Sara's hands. 'Well, and how's
my girl? You're looking gorgeous, sweetheart. Do I get
a kiss in greeting too?' His arms slid round her and he
bent his head and kissed her before she realised what
he meant to do, and there was the smell of whisky on
his breath. The celebration had evidently started already.

Jason had detached himself from Diana. 'Are we all
ready?' he asked rather brusquely. 'Your car or mine,
Oliver?'

'Mine, boyo. Plenty of bubbly stashed away in the back. Can't have a launching without bubbly, can we?' He guffawed. 'You two lovebirds pile in the back. Sara will come in front and hold my hand while I drive.'

Jason stood without moving. 'I never trust myself to a one-handed driver,' he said, and he wasn't smiling.

Oliver gave him an uncertain look. 'Oh, come *on*, Jason. Only my little joke!'

Diana's full-throated laugh rang down the quiet street. 'Ollie's sense of humour is positively *criminal*! Come on, darling Jay.' She took Jason's hand and urged him towards the red car. 'It'll be a bit of a squash, but we won't mind, will we?' She flashed a smile at him, all white teeth and red lips.

Sara climbed in beside Oliver. 'That's right, sweetheart, snuggle close.' He gave her a squeeze as his hand went to the self-starter and the car roared away down the street.

The harbour front was only minutes away. They parked the car and walked along the quayside. Oliver and Sara in front, one of his arms round Sara and the other hand swinging a wicker carrier from which protruded the tops of the champagne bottles.

'This is jolly!' He lowered his head to plant a kiss on her hair. 'Something to celebrate, eh?'

Sara wasn't sure there was. She didn't like the way the evening was shaping. Trying to change the atmosphere, she looked up and down the old quayside, with its harbour offices and ships' chandlers—closed up and looking faintly mysterious in the early evening light—and thought it couldn't have changed all that much since pirates had flourished here long ago.

She said, 'It all looks so old. You could almost expect to meet a smuggler in a red stocking cap with a patch over one eye.'

It wasn't the most tactful of remarks, she realised as soon as she had made it. Oliver slid her a ghoulish look and whispered close to her ear, 'Once aboard the lugger and the girl is mine, eh?' He giggled foolishly.

From behind, Jason's voice, sounding rather curt, said, 'We've left her pulled into the harbour wall just for tonight, Oliver. She'll be at her moorings tomorrow, if that's what you want.'

'Just as you say, chum,' Oliver replied. 'Here she is, the beauty. Let's get aboard!' He jumped clumsily down and held out his arms for Sara, but Jason pushed past her and then guided her down the iron ladder in the harbour wall. Diana followed, laughing away Jason's helping hand, as if to underline the breezy, lively personality she was projecting. Jason was a strong man, a man of action; he would want a girl who could match him, Sara thought unhappily.

Lying afloat, the yacht seemed smaller than when it had towered above her in the boatyard, but Sara could see that it was a very luxurious craft indeed. Diana and Jason were immediately immersed in discussions about the electric winch, the way the cockpit roof rolled back, the new type of hand-held compass. It all meant nothing to Sara, who trailed round with Oliver, trying not to notice the two in front, their heads close together, the dark one and the golden one with its smart nautical cap perched on top.

Oliver said rather ruefully at last, 'Afraid I don't know much about the workings. Diana's the expert—I just pay the bills.' Suddenly his large fair face looked downcast. 'The boat was Diana's idea and she always gets what she wants.' He looked towards the other two, standing close to examine something in the cockpit, and at that moment Jason's arm closed round Diana's shoulders and they bent down together, her face lifted to his, her mouth inviting. 'See what I mean?' added Oliver, and Sara looked away quickly. 'Made for each other, those two!'

She was horribly afraid he was right. Diana was Jason's kind of girl and she, Sara, was just a helpless child, who up to now had let everyone push her around. All that had to change, she vowed. She was better now, she would get away as soon as she could and forget about Jason Knight, and be her own girl.

They went down to the cabin, beautifully fitted, all teak and softly upholstered berths. There was a built-in cocktail cabinet, a selection of lockers ready to be filled, even a tiny television set. Adjoining was a tiny kitchen (or galley, as Diana insisted on calling it) and further again, a second sleeping compartment with two more berths.

'It's *exactly* as I imagined it, Jay,' Diana enthused. 'You are a clever darling, to build us such a super boat. Come on, now, let's drink to her.' She laughed her high, ringing laugh. 'I'm not going to waste a bottle of champagne by launching her in the official way—we'll drink the bubby instead!' She pulled a bottle out of the wicker carrier and began to unwrap the glasses. 'Oh, Oliver, you chump, you've broken one when you did your circus act, jumping down on to the deck. Never mind, Jay and I will share, won't we, darling?'

The bottles were opened, the corks popping, the wine foaming on to the carpeted floor; toasts were drunk to the new boat called *Diana*. Then Jason toasted 'the other Diana, who thought it all up' and she laughed and kissed him, and they drank champagne from the same glass.

The light was fading now, and down in the cabin things were looking shadowed and dusky. The gas bottles, Jason told them, weren't yet connected so they couldn't light up. 'There's a torch somewhere,' he said. 'I think I left it through here.' He walked through the kitchen into the other sleeping compartment, followed by Diana. There was the sound of giggling from Diana and some scuffling, and then silence. They didn't return.

Oliver had been drinking silently and steadily. Now he pulled Sara down on to the soft bed. 'A bit narrow, I'm afraid, sweetheart.' He hiccuped slightly. 'We shouldn't have let them have the best one, through there.'

He drew her against him. He had discarded the reefer jacket he had been wearing and his body felt hot and damp through his shirt. His breath spoke eloquently of the amount of drink he had had. Sara drew away distastefully.

'Ah, don't be like that, girlie. I know you've had'— he hiccuped again—'bad time, but life's got to go on, y'know. No good dwelling on the past.' He reached out and fumbled with the buttons of her blouse.

She pushed him away. 'No, *please*, Oliver,' she whispered desperately. She didn't want to make a scene— not with those two so near, in the next compartment— but Oliver's closeness was repugnant to her. 'Let me go!'

She began to struggle, but he pulled her closer until she was lying on the bed beside him. She started to cry out, but his mouth clamped on to hers, stopping her voice. His hand was groping inside her blouse now and she could feel his soft body shaking all over.

Suddenly there was the white light of a powerful torch on them, and Jason's shadow loomed in the doorway. He stood for a moment, silently, then he said in an expressionless voice, 'Break it up, you two, we're leaving now.'

Taken by surprise, Oliver slackened his grip and Sara wriggled out of his arms and stood up. trying to evade the beam of the torch while she fastened her blouse. Her body was burning all over and all she wanted to do was to jump off the boat and sink to the bottom of the harbour.

Oliver lumbered to his feet. 'Not exactly tactful, was it, ole man?' He lurched where he stood and grabbed at the locker over the bed, and Jason said,

'I think we'd better get you home, hadn't we?'

Behind him, Diana cried gaily, 'Let's all go back to our place and put on some records and fix ourselves something out of the fridge.'

Everything inside Sara revolted as she guessed the way the rest of the evening was going to turn out. She didn't wait to hear what Jason said. She turned and ran up the steps to the deck. All she wanted to do was to get away from Oliver Forbes and his beautiful yacht and his beastly sister. She was almost in tears as she put her foot impetuously on the bottom rung of the iron ladder and began to climb up the wet, seaweedy harbour wall.

She had only managed to pull herself up two steep rungs when her foot slipped. She grabbed wildly at the rail but, taken by surprise, lost her balance and swung out sideways, holding on by one hand. She heard a shout, but it was too late. The next thing she knew was that she was crumpled up on the deck of the yacht and Jason was bending over her.

'Sara, what a damn fool thing to do! Why didn't you wait for us?' He sounded furiously angry, but his touch was gentle as he went down on one knee, flexing her legs, her ankles. 'Does that hurt? Have you broken anything?'

'I—I don't think so.' She sat up carefully. Then she had the brainwave. 'It's just—just my ankle.' She moaned as he touched it; if she was going to put on an act she might as well do it as convincingly as she could. 'I think I must have twisted it.'

Diana stood looking down at her. 'Stand up and try your weight on it,' she said coldly. 'You'll soon know if you're really hurt.' She sounded annoyed, and of course this would spoil her plans for the evening, Sara thought with satisfaction.

Clinging to Jason's hand, one of his arms round her waist, she struggled to her feet. Her ankle felt a little stiff, but there was no piercing pain, no pain of any sort. But she let out a little squeal. 'Oh dear! I'm afraid it *is* rather painful.'

She felt Jason's arms close round her more tightly, taking all her weight, and she leaned heavily against him. It was bliss to be in his arms, even if he was only being kind, as he had been on the train. Ruefully she thought that the only way to assuage this awful hunger she felt for him was to stage some sort of crisis. It would be funny if it weren't so heartbreaking.

He said, 'I'd better get you back home straight away so I can see what the damage is. It's no use trying to examine it here, with no lighting on.'

'Oh, but surely there's no need to take her home.' Diana sound pettish. 'Bring her back to our place and our housekeeper can bind it up for her, or something.'

'Thanks, Diana, but we'll do it my way.' Jason's tone was pleasant but allowed no argument. 'Can you manage to scramble on to my back, Sara, and I'll hoist you up to the quayside.' He turned round. 'Put your feet into my hands.'

He lifted her without difficulty and she clung round his neck, her face buried in the thick dark hair, He climbed the iron ladder easily and lowered her to the ground. 'As light as a feather,' he said with a grin. 'Now, wait here while I dash off and fetch my car.'

Diana had joined them now, and Oliver was making his way up the ladder, panting slightly. 'Couldn't Oliver take her home?' Diana wasn't giving up easily. 'Isn't your aunt there to look after her?'

Jason shook his head. 'Aunt Vera's out visiting friends.' He glanced towards the edge of the wall, where Oliver's head was appearing, swaying unsteadily. 'And in any case I doubt if Oliver is capable of driving anyone anywhere just at the moment,' he added drily. 'I'd advise you to take the wheel yourself, Diana.'

She stared at him for a moment, evidently undecided whether to sulk or not, and then decided against. 'Oh well, it was nice while it lasted,' she smiled meaningly into Jason's eyes. 'We'll see you at the yard tomorrow for the final arrangements.'

'O.K.,' shouted Jason, already running away from them along the quayside.

Diana stared down at Sara, sitting in a heap on the stone. 'Do you want us to wait until he comes back?' she said ungraciously.

'Oh no, please don't trouble, I'll be quite all right. Goodnight, and thank you for the party.' She didn't look in Oliver's direction.

'Some party!' sneered Diana. 'Come on, goofy, let's get you into the car.' She grabbed her brother's arm and led him, protesting vaguely, towards the red car, pushing him into the passenger seat without ceremony. It was quite obviously not the first time she had done this particular service for him. With a sigh of the utmost relief Sara watched them drive away. Now she had to wait for Jason to come back and she didn't look forward to that. She had spoilt the party for him, too.

But when he drove up a few minutes later there were no recriminations. He helped her into the car, not roughly but not with particular care either, and she didn't attempt to carry on the charade by wincing or crying out. Jason would find out soon enough that she hadn't hurt herself at all—and then the trouble would begin.

He got in behind the wheel. 'Quite comfortable, you poor darling?' he said, with a nasty edge to his voice.

'Yes, thank you,' she whispered, fastening the safety belt hastily and sliding as far away from him as possible.

They had driven a couple of miles in complete silence when Sara realised that they were not going back the way they had come. 'Aren't we going over the ferry, then?' she asked.

'No, we're going the long way round,' he said blandly. 'It's a nice evening for a drive.'

'But you said you—you wanted to get me back home to——'

'To examine the sprained ankle that never was?'

'How did you know?' she said in a small voice.

'I hadn't any doubt at all. You never even flinched when I moved it at first. You were putting on an act. Why, Sara?'

'I didn't want to go back to the Forbes' home.'

He kept his eyes on the road ahead, but in the pale glimmer from the car lights she saw his eyebrows go up thoughtfully.

They drove in silence for a long time. Sara was occupied by the thought that he didn't appear to be disappointed that the party at the Forbes' house hadn't happened. It was a little thing, it didn't solve any of her problems, but she hugged the thought to her as if he had presented her with a priceless gift.

They drove through Wareham in the evening quiet, and along the Swanage road. At Corfe Castle Jason said, 'We'll go over the hills. There's a place up there where you can pull in and get a wonderful view.'

He meant to park the car and look at the view—and then what? Her heart began to beat faster and nervousness made her say idiotically, 'Really? Is that all part of the tour schedule, and do I tip the driver?'

'Don't be sarcastic, Sara,' he said crisply. 'It doesn't suit you.'

There was very little on the narrow road. They switchbacked up and down the hills without meeting more than two or three cars. Finally, at the top of a long hill, the road opened out to the left of them, with a wide pull-in for perhaps a dozen or so cars. But in April they were the only ones there.

Jason parked the car and switched off the engine and the lights. Sara stared down at the breathtaking view spread out in front and far below. It wasn't quite dark yet and, with the car lights off, she could see the whole length of the sea channel stretching from Poole Harbour almost to Wareham. The water gleamed like polished steel and the lights of the houses and buildings looked like glow-worms in the distance. White mist came up in wisps from the fields and heath all around. She glanced at Jason, sitting very still beside her, and could sense the tension in him.

'It—it's very beautiful up here,' she said, and her voice wasn't quite steady.

'Yes,' he said, 'but I didn't bring you here to look at the view. We have to talk and this is a good place. Aunt Vera may be home by now.' He released his seatbelt and sat back in his corner so that he could watch her in the dusk. 'First of all,' he said, 'tell me exactly why you didn't want to go back to the Forbes'.'

'Because I didn't want to be landed with Oliver. He was quite drunk and I didn't like the way he was behaving.'

'No? You didn't look as if you were objecting very strongly when I turned the flashlight on you.'

'Appearances can be deceptive,' she said coldly. 'And you always judge by appearances, don't you?'

'Are you trying to pick a quarrel with me, Sara?'

A week ago—back in that other world, that other life—she would have quailed before the sternness of his voice. But no longer. She shrugged. 'I don't really care very much. If you want to quarrel, I'm ready.'

'I don't,' he said with surprising mildness. 'So—you weren't leading him on, then? He's a very rich man, as I told you.'

Her temper flared. 'Oh, shut up about money. Can't you think of anything else?'

'Lots of things,' he mocked. Then, 'Well, if you weren't exactly hooked on Oliver why didn't you make a fuss? You could have screamed.'

'Because I was considering *you*,' she shot at him venomously. 'After all, they're your friends, not mine. I didn't want to embarrass you.'

'Oh, not my friends, I assure you. Merely customers.'

'Do you usually take your lady customers into a dark cabin and—and stay there?' She regretted the words almost before they were out.

'Ah, I see,' he said softly. 'So that's it, is it?'

'That's what?'

'Oh, nothing. Just a thought.'

The silence that followed lasted so long that Sara began to feel suffocated. She put a hand to her throat. 'Was that all you brought me up here to talk about?'

'No,' he said slowly, in the deep voice that stirred something inside her almost painfully. 'It occurs to me that we seem doomed to misunderstand each other about almost everything. I think the time has come for you to tell me the whole story, everything that led up to your marrying Tim, and what happened afterwards. You keep on saying I've misjudged you. Well, prove it.'

This was what she had longed for, but now the moment had arrived she was petrified. 'But will you believe me?' she sighed. 'Or will you just throw it back in my face, the way you've done with everything I've said since I first met you?'

'I don't know,' he said flatly. 'It's a risk you have to take.'

She could hardly breathe. Releasing the catch of the safety-belt, she sat back with a long, long sigh. If she told him the truth and he still didn't believe her, it was the end—the bitter, bitter end, and she would leave his house tomorrow and never see him again.

But if she was afraid to take the risk then she would have lost the one flimsy hope she had.

'All right,' she said. 'I'll tell you.'

And sitting there, high up in the hills, with the twinkling lights far below, and the darkness all around, she told him. She told him about her father's early death, her mother's marriage to Ralph.

'I think we must have been fairly well off. We lived in a nice house outside London when I was very young. I remember it well—it had a big garden. But after my mother remarried everything changed. I was sent away to school, and soon after that they told me that my mother had died. I wanted to die, too, for a while, but I was only seven and I suppose I got over it fairly soon.'

'Your stepfather looked after you? Came to visit you?'

'He came once,' she said, 'and told me that I would have to stay at school for good, that he couldn't take me to live with him. I hadn't any aunts or uncles or anyone, I was quite alone. He said there was only just enough money to keep me at school and I wasn't to expect anything more from him.'

'So he paid for your schooling?'

She shook her head. 'I found out—years afterwards—that my real father had taken out an insurance policy for my schooling when I was born. So I didn't really owe Ralph anything. And I didn't see him again for years.'

She told him how Ralph had turned up again when she was almost due to leave school; how he had taken her to live with him and travel with him to the glamorous resorts; how he had bought her clothes and showed her off to his acquaintances.

'I never guessed what he was really like,' she said in a whisper. 'He said, at the end, that I was "green", and I think I must have been. You don't learn a lot about life at school. You think you know it all, but of course you don't. He was so charming to me, and fun to be with, and everyone liked him. But he didn't like me to meet young men and he always scared them off. He said he didn't want me to fall in love and leave him alone just yet, and I believed him. Then, in Acapulco, I met Tim.'

She was silent for so long that Jason said at last in a grim voice, 'Go on.'

'Well, Tim—he—he fell in love with me. He asked me to marry him, or at least agree to a sort of secret engagement, but I told him it was out of the question. I liked him so much, but I wasn't in love with him. I didn't know what love was.' She turned her head quickly. 'What did you say?'

'Nothing. Go on.'

She drew a long breath before she went on about the visit to Carlos Sorano's home in Mexico City, about the odd, frightened feeling she had begun to get about the whole thing. 'I thought of him as an old man,' she said, 'I never dreamed what was going to happen. He showed me his house and he told me his wife had died the year before. I felt sorry for him. Then he took me out into the garden. It was like a jungle and he had a clearing where he had built a kind of model of a Mayan temple and he told me about the human sacrifices his ancestors used to make. And—and there was a huge model of a jaguar god.' She shuddered. 'It terrified me.'

'I should bloody well think it did,' broke in Jason violently. 'And then what? What happened then?'

'Nothing, really, until we got back to the hotel in Acapulco. Then Ralph told me that Carlos wanted to marry me. Ralph—he—he changed completely. I hardly knew him. He said he was broke to the wide and if I didn't agree to do as he said he would just disappear— "go to ground", he said—and leave me alone there, without money or—or anyone to help. He locked me in my room and left me to make up my mind.'

'Then Tim found you?'

'Yes,' she said. 'He found out where I was and got hold of a key from the office and came up. I suppose I was in a bit of a state. I didn't want to tell him at first—it was all so—so degrading. But he got it out of me and he said he would take me away and we would be married, so that Ralph wouldn't be able to find me and—and use me for his own purposes. I think I was a bit unhinged by then. I was so scared I didn't know what I was doing. Anyway, Tim took charge of me and he was wonderful, he thought of everything. We were married next day in Mexico City and then—well, you know the rest.'

Into the blank silence that followed she said in a tiny, shaken voice, 'He did love me, Jason, and I—I liked him so much, I would have loved him in the end, I'm sure I would. I'd have given him anything.'

She sat staring ahead out of the windscreen, and all the light below blurred into one, as tears swam into her eyes.

There, it was done—it was all said, and if he didn't believe her she could do no more.

At last he said in an odd voice, 'And how much *did* you give him?'

She shook her bent head. 'Nothing. I gave him nothing at all. There wasn't time, you see.'

'You mean—you and Tim, you didn't sleep together?'

She lifted her head wearily. 'Is it important?'

'Yes,' he said, 'it's important to me.'

'Well then, we didn't. He said I was tired and he—he wouldn't bother me.' She began to sob quietly, pressing her fist against her lips like a child.

Jason waited until she had quietened, then he said evenly, 'So there was no plot to get hold of some of the Knight family fortune, such as it is?'

She shook her head. 'I didn't even know there *was* a family fortune. Is there?'

'Oh yes, there is,' he said, rather as if he were talking about some other family. 'My father inherited quite a pile from his father and he put it all into our boatbuilding firm. When he died, ten years ago, he left the lot equally divided between Tim and me. Tim's share—which you could claim now, of course, as his widow—will amount to a considerable sum of money. If you decide to take it out of the business it may leave me in something of a difficulty. I've been stretching our finance quite a bit lately, putting money into expansion, with a view to stepping up our overseas trade. That's why we were in Mexico.'

Sara blinked, trying to take it all in. 'But I wouldn't,'

she said. 'I wouldn't dream of taking Tim's money, it wouldn't be fair.'

'Being fair isn't very fashionable these days,' he said drily. 'Especially when money's involved.'

'I wouldn't touch Tim's money,' she said stubbornly.

Jason lay back in the corner of the seat and she could feel his eyes on her in the near-darkness. 'So,' he said at last. 'That's your story, is it? No plot? No arrangement to meet up with your rather disgusting stepfather and share out the loot?'

'No,' she said. 'No arrangement. I hope I'll never see Ralph again as long as I live.'

He didn't move or speak. In the glimmer of light that reached the car their eyes met across a silence that seemed to vibrate with tension. Sara held her breath until it seemed that her chest would burst. She stared at the pale blur of his face and the strange, grey-green glitter of his eyes and felt her heartbeat quicken until it was choking her. She began to tremble.

Then he said huskily, 'I *want* to believe you. God, how I want to! You've got under my skin, Sara, you and your beautiful little face and your hair like sunlight and your body that was made for love. I wanted you the first time I saw you, and you've tormented me ever since.'

Sara felt the heat surging through her. He wanted her, he loved her. In another moment he would move towards her, take her in his arms. Her lips parted softly as if his own lips were on them already. Her hunger for him was so intense that she felt as if she were falling towards him.

She heard his harsh intake of breath. Then her world seemed to be falling apart as he stretched out his hand with a quick, jerky movement and turned the key in the self-starter. 'If I touch you now,' he said between his teeth, 'I won't know where to stop. We'll get back home.'

He drove the last few miles with furious concentration, leaning forward a little, his eyes fixed on the narrow road, his hands clenched on the wheel. Sara lay back in her seat, dazed with happiness. He loved her and she could wait for his kisses. There was all their life ahead of them. She hugged her arms round her body, lost in a haze of well-being that follows a time of unbearable tension.

They drove through the darkened village, past the cottages and little houses with lights at their windows; then down the lane towards the sea and turned in at the grey stone house that seemed to have a new, welcoming look now that she wouldn't have to leave it.

Aunt Vera was at home and had heard the car. She came out on to the step as Jason and Sara walked towards the front door.

'My dears, I'm so glad you're back early,' she said, and Sara caught the anxious note in her voice that was usually so calm and placid. 'I've only been home a short time and I found a car waiting here when the taxi dropped me. There's a man called who says he's your stepfather, Sara. A Mr Francis, he said his name was. I didn't quite know what to do, but he said you were expecting him, so I asked him in. He's waiting for you in the sitting room.' She went back into the house and down the hall towards the kitchen.

Ralph was sitting at his ease in one of the comfortable chintzy chairs in the sitting room, leafing through one of Jason's yachting magazines. He wore a brown tweed suit and he looked prosperous and cheerful. He stood up unhurriedly as Sara came into the room, followed by Jason.

'Sara, my poor dear girl! You have led me a dance!'

The charming, crooked smile, the depreciating tone of voice. Seeing him, hearing him, Sara felt sick.

Her hands were cold and limp with shock and he took them in both his hands and looked deep into her eyes. Gently chiding, he said, 'Why did you feel you had to elope like that, you foolish romantic child? And then the tragedy! I had to piece it together bit by bit and it's taken me all this time. Why didn't you come back to me?—you knew I'd understand.'

She swallowed with difficulty, one hand to her throat. 'Ralph, you shouldn't have come here. I didn't want to see you.'

Jason's voice, from behind her, said icily. 'That is my sentiment entirely, Mr Francis. I must make it plain that you're not welcome in my house and I'd be glad if you'd leave immediately.'

Ralph registered hurt bewilderment. 'But, my dear boy, why on earth—'

'You heard what I said. I don't have to justify it.' Jason looked at a spot between Sara's eyes and his face was carved in stone. 'If you want to leave with your stepfather, Sara, perhaps he'd wait in his car until you've packed your things. On the other hand, if you want to stay until tomorrow, you're welcome.'

He turned and walked to the door. There he paused briefly. 'You'll need my solicitor's address in Poole. You'll find it in the telephone book. Bryant and Bryant is the name.'

Sara came to life. She ran after him and caught him as he opened the front door.

She grabbed his arm. 'Jason, please stop! It isn't what you think, I didn't ask him to come. I didn't expect him—'

His expression froze the words on her lips. 'There've been enough lies,' he said. 'You've had a good teacher.'

He put a hand to the latch and his mouth curled in the contemptuous smile she knew so well, but had almost forgotten in these last few days.

'And I so nearly believed you,' he said, and he went out and closed the door. A moment later she heard his car start up and the crunch of gravel as he drove away down the drive.

## CHAPTER EIGHT

SARA went back into the sitting room. Ralph was standing by a side table, pouring himself a drink. He grinned at her, lifting his glass. 'Has he gone? Phew! that's a hard nut, that brother-in-law of yours.'

She said in a high, clear voice, 'You heard what he said, and this is his house. You'd better go.'

'But you married his brother—surely he wouldn't——' He looked at her face and stopped. Then, in a smooth, reasonable voice, he began again. 'Look, darling, this is really all rather immature and over-dramatic, don't you think? Why can't we just sit down and talk it over, you and I? It was all a misunderstanding, about old Carlos, you know. I soon saw that it wouldn't have done at all. And actually, you've done pretty well for yourself by marrying that poor young blighter Knight. I'd no idea at the time there was so much money floating around in his family.' His glance roamed over the large, well-appointed room with its early English oak furniture, its original watercolour paintings, its large Persian rug before the fireplace. He grinned knowingly. 'I always said you'd make a beautiful widow, didn't I?'

Sara's control snapped. She snatched the glass of

whisky out of his hand and threw it to the floor, where it lay dribbling out its contents on to the polished wood. 'Get out!' she snapped. 'Get out now, and keep out of my life. I never want to see you again.'

He looked down at the broken glass ruefully. 'All right, all right, my dear, so you're upset. I'm sorry, I'll go now. But you won't want to stay long here, not with that fellow who just went out. A nasty bit of work if ever I saw one! Here's an address that will find me for the next week or two.' He tore a sheet from a notebook and placed it on the back of a chair. 'Just phone me and we can get together again.'

'Goodbye, Ralph,' she said coldly.

At last she had got through to him. 'Oh, well——' He shrugged, with a flamboyant gesture of both hands. 'C'est la vie!' He walked out of the room with a slight swagger in his step.

Sara followed him to the front door and stood watching until his car had turned the corner of the drive and the sound of it had died away.

Aunt Vera came into the hall as Sara closed the door. 'Where is everybody?' She pushed back her curly brown hair in a flustered way. 'Has your stepfather gone? I thought he might be staying overnight, so I was just going up to get the spare room ready.'

'He had to go,' Sara said, and smiled. Now that it was all over it was extraordinary how calm she felt. 'Jason went out again too. I think he was going back to the Forbes', they were carrying on the launching party at their home, but I didn't feel much like it, so Jason very kindly drove me back here.' She went into the sitting room. 'I'm terribly sorry, Aunt Vera, but my stepfather had an accident with one of your glasses. I do hope it wasn't a very valuable one. I'll get the dustpan and brush it up.'

She went on chattering while she brushed up the broken glass and mopped over the floor. 'I'll re-polish it in the morning,' she said brightly, 'if Mrs Gardner doesn't turn up again.'

She stood up, straightening her back as if it were aching. Aunt Vera put a hand on her arm. 'Sara dear,' she said gently, 'something's the matter. What's happened?'

'Nothing. Nothing, really. Everything's fine.' Sara smiled brilliantly.

The older woman sighed. 'Oh well, never mind. But you look absolutely fagged out. You go straight up to bed and I'll bring you a hot drink.'

'That would be lovely,' said Sara, 'you really do spoil me.' She took the mop back into the kitchen. Her limbs felt as if they belonged to a jointed doll. She got herself into bed and presently Aunt Vera brought up a milky drink and sat on the side of the bed while Sara rattled on about the launching of the *Diana*. The words seemed to come out by themselves, for inside there was nothing but blank emptiness. She didn't want to think or feel, or plan. Just to get away from here before she saw Jason again, that was all that was important.

Finally, when she couldn't think of anything else to say, there was an awkward little pause and Vera Knight got up to go. Impulsively Sara blurted out, 'Aunt Vera, I'm afraid I'll have to leave you tomorrow.'

'Oh dear, that's rather a blow. I thought—I hoped—— But of course you'll be joining your stepfather. I didn't realise you had any relatives. Jason didn't tell me.' The grey eyes under the curly brown hair were puzzled.

Sara didn't answer that. She said, 'You've been so very kind to me. I'll be sorry to go.'

'But you'll come back and see us often—stay with us?'

'Oh yes, of course, I'd love to.' Never, never, her dulled brain told her.

She knew that Aunt Vera was waiting, hoping for something more, some explanation perhaps, but the words would have choked her. She had meant to tell her the whole story, perhaps to enlist her sympathy and understanding, but that was impossible now. She said apologetically, leaning back against the pillow, 'I believe you were right. I really do feel awfully tired now.'

Aunt Vera nodded sagely. 'I thought so.' She pulled the duvet over Sara, picked up the empty mug and then bent and kissed her cheek. 'Sleep well, my dear, bless you,' she said, and went out and shut the door quietly.

It was the first night of her life that Sara didn't sleep at all. Even that awful night in Mexico City, with Jason on the other side of the communicating door, she had slept eventually. But not tonight. Here, his bedroom was on the far side of the house, but she would hear his car come back. She had no clear idea what she meant to do when she heard him come in, but she had a feeling that only when she had seen him again would this tight band that gripped her head like steel relax its pressure. She sat in a chair beside the window, shivering, although she had the duvet wrapped round her, and watched the dawn over the sea, grey and chill, and Jason didn't come home all night.

When it was light she washed and dressed herself in the coral trouser suit with the white blouse. Then she packed her few belongings in the travelling valise that Jason had bought for her in Mexico City. Every single thing she owned had been paid for by Jason Knight, she thought bleakly, and resolved to repay every penny when she had some money.

At nine o'clock she went downstairs and made herself a cup of coffee. The house was quiet and deserted. Mrs

Gardner, the daily help, didn't come until ten, if she came at all. Aunt Vera always took her own breakfast tray up to her room the night before and made coffee when she wakened. She had, she had told Vera, a slight problem with raised blood pressure and had been advised by her doctor to take it easy when she could.

As Sara was going upstairs again the morning post dropped through the letter box on to the tiled hall floor. She glanced idly at it. Nothing for her, of course, it was too soon for Miss Glyn to contact her.

But there was a letter and it was from Miss Glyn. 'You will be surprised to hear from me so soon, Sara,' the headmistress wrote, 'but after you left today an idea occurred to me which might appeal to you. It is going to be impossible for you to start on a secretarial course at the College half-way through a term, but we could certainly use some help in the office here at school. Our secretary is overwhelmed with work just at present, and if you would care to come and lend a hand I'm sure we should both be most grateful. I could fix up a room for you and you would have your board and a small salary, and you would be able to begin to pick up some office routine. Let me know if this appeals to you. Yours sincerely, L. Glyn.'

Sara took the letter up to her room and placed it carefully in her handbag. It would be a relief to have somewhere definite to go and something definite to work on, but she didn't want to leave anything lying around that would give a clue to her whereabouts. It was going to be a clean break.

She went down the passage and knocked on the door at the end. Aunt Vera was sitting up in bed drinking coffee. She smiled at Sara so warmly and affectionately that just for a moment her resolve almost weakened. But she couldn't let that happen. She said, 'I came to say goodbye. I'm just off to catch the Bournemouth bus.'

Vera Knight's smile faded. 'Oh dear, I didn't think you'd be leaving so early, Sara, or I'd have been up and dressed to see you off. Just throw me over my dressing gown, there's a dear child. Have you had some breakfast?'

Sara assured her that she had, and went back to her room for her case. Just for a minute she allowed herself to stay, looking round the comfortable room with its view out over the sea, thinking that this was the nearest thing to a real home she remembered. Then she closed the door and went downstairs.

Aunt Vera was standing in the hall. 'I hate to see you rushing away like this, dear. You're sure you'll be all right?' Her hand fluttered agitatedly at the girdle of her blue dressing gown. 'You'll be getting a train in Bournemouth, will you? Your stepfather is in London, is he?'

'Yes,' said Sara truthfully, adding hastily, in case Aunt Vera asked for an address, 'I'll give you a ring as soon as I arrive.'

'Oh yes, please do that, dear.' She glanced at Sara's pale face. 'Jason knows that you're going, of course? He didn't come in last night— I looked into his room on the way down. He must have stayed with the Forbes.'

'Oh yes, he knows I'm going,' said Sara. 'We arranged it yesterday.' *If you want to stay until tomorrow, you're welcome.* Just remembering the way he had looked when he said that sent an icy tremor through her already cold body.

Vera Knight put her arms round Sara and kissed her. 'Hurry then, dear, if you *must* catch that bus. I do wish,' she added wistfully, 'that you didn't have to go.'

At the gate Sara turned and waved, thinking sadly that if she had ever really known her mother she might have been like Vera Knight. That would have been wonderful.

As soon as she reached the school Sara went straight to the headmistress's study and tapped on the door. There was no answer, so she stood outside and waited, pretending not to notice the interested glances of the second-formers who poured out of the gym past the study door. 'Ooh, trendy!' she heard one of them giggle to her neighbour in a whisper, staring at Sara's coral trouser suit, her scarlet sandals and shining gold hair.

Miss Glyn appeared then, a slightly awe-inspiring figure, with the black gown she always wore in class floating about her. 'Ah, Sara Tildesley! Come in, Sara.'

Sara followed her into the study and took the chair indicated, feeling like a schoolgirl again. 'So you got my letter?' Miss Glyn said, and Sara replied shyly,

'Yes, thank you, Miss Glyn. I'm very grateful and I'd like to come and start straight away, if I may?'

'You certainly may. We have a rush on and poor Miss Barrett is complaining bitterly—University Entrance, you know. You won't know our present secretary, Miss Barrett. She's new since your time. I'll take you along and introduce you.' She looked a little doubtfully at the coral trouser suit. 'Or perhaps you'd better change first. I'll ask Matron to see about a room for you. It will have to be up on the top floor and very small, I'm afraid.'

'Oh, yes,' said Sara eagerly. 'That will do beautifully.'

Miss Glyn looked hard at her and her austere expression softened a little. 'Things have been going wrong for you, Sara? You've had a bad time?'

Sara nodded, her mouth trembling. 'Everything went wrong. It's a long story and you won't have time to hear it, but—but I ought to tell you that I'm not Sara Tildesley any longer. I'm Sara Knight now. I was married in Mexico quite a short time ago and my—my husband was killed in a train crash the same day. I was in hospital for a while, but I wasn't badly hurt. Just shock, and a bang on the head, they told me.'

Miss Glyn looked very grave. 'You poor child! How tragic for you!' There was a pause and then she asked the inevitable question. 'You're not pregnant, are you?'

Sara shook her head. 'Oh, no. It's just that for—various reasons I haven't any money and nowhere to go just at present.'

Miss Glyn nodded and drew a writing pad towards her. 'Your married name is Knight, you said?' She wrote it down.

Sara said rather timidly, 'Would you mind if I didn't speak of it to anyone? I'd rather be known as Sara Tildesley to the people here who remember me. I'll take off my wedding ring.'

'Very well, if you prefer it, Sara.'

'And—and perhaps you would let me look through the lost property and see if I can find something to wear that isn't likely to be claimed.' She glanced down wryly at the coral trouser suit. 'This isn't very suitable, is it?'

'Hardly.' Miss Glyn smiled, and—coming from Miss Glyn—the smile was warming and sympathetic. 'Run along then, you know where everything is.'

'Oh yes. And thank you so very much. This is a lifeline for me.' Sara felt the headmistress's eyes fixed thoughtfully on her as she went out of the study.

School was a haven and a hiding place. Work was a drug. For the fortnight up to the end of the Easter term work filled every waking moment. In the daytime she sat at a small desk in the school secretary's office. Miss

Barrett was a brisk, sandy woman in enormous thick-rimmed glasses, pleasant enough to work with but not someone to confide in, even if there had been time for confidences—which there wasn't.

Sara quickly picked up the filing, and taught herself to type with two fingers of each hand. She ran innumerable errands for Miss Barrett to all parts of the school. It helped that she knew every inch of the old building by heart.

All her contemporaries had left the previous summer, but many of the younger girls remembered her and gave her rather curious looks when they came into the secretary's office. Members of the staff had a kind word for her, evidently having been informed by Miss Glyn that 'something had gone wrong for Sara Tildesley', but they were all madly busy with the annual rush of University Entrance, and they hadn't much time to bother with the pale young girl in the grey skirt and white blouse, her fair hair tied back with a ribbon, who sat in the corner of the office with her back to the room. She had taken off her wedding ring and hung it round her neck on a ribbon, and as she wore the old school blouse buttoned up to the neck it didn't show.

It felt very odd to be wearing school uniform again after all the glamorous clothes she had worn in the past year, but the white blouse and grey skirt and cardigan were all she could find in the lost property cupboard that fitted her, so they would have to do for the present. When she got her first monthly salary cheque she would venture out into the town and buy a plain dress. The very thought that she might encounter Jason in Poole kept her away from the town at present. Her inside turned over sickly at the thought that she might suddenly see him.

It was a pale, twilit life. Sometimes she felt as if she

had grown a shell around her and that nothing could touch her or make her feel alive again. This had been the plan she had thought out—to come and ask Miss Glyn for help and advice—and it had worked out splendidly, she told herself. As soon as she had saved enough she would find out about secretarial courses. Perhaps Miss Dunn, the careers mistress, would help her about getting a grant, when the end of term rush was over. She would put in for a place at a college somewhere right away from here; London perhaps, or Bristol, or Birmingham. Somewhere huge, where she could bury herself away, safe from the chance of ever running into Jason Knight again. She was determined to wipe him out of her mind and out of her life. She knew she had a fight on her hands and it was worst at night, on the nights when she couldn't sleep. Sometimes the longing to see him and touch him and feel his hands on her was so urgent and intolerable that she got out of bed and paced the tiny room, just as she had done that night in Mexico City. But now he wasn't on the other side of the door. What would have happened, she wondered, if she had turned the handle that night and gone in to him?

The term ended in the usual flurry of writing reports, with most of the staff looking demented; of the school concert and the school play; of interviews with parents and a line of cars up the drive.

But at last the old house was quiet. The last 'See you next term' had echoed along the corridors, the last car door had slammed. It was all so familiar to Sara, but now she was seeing it from the background.

There wasn't a single girl left behind to spend the holiday at school as she had always spent it, except once or twice when she had been invited to visit the homes of friends. Most of the staff had left, but the careers mistress was still here, tidying up odds and ends. Sara planned to approach her now.

But before she could do that Miss Glyn sent for her— a more relaxed and human Miss Glyn, now that school term was over—but Sara still felt the old sinking feeling that accompanied being sent for by the headmistress.

'Well, Sara, sit down and tell me how you've been enjoying yourself. Miss Barrett tells me that you've been a great help.'

'I've enjoyed it very much,' Sara said politely. 'And I think I've learned quite a bit.'

'Good—and have you any plans now?'

'I was going to see Miss Dunn and ask her advice about the possibility of my getting a grant.'

'Yes. Well, before you do anything about that I think you should read this.' Miss Glyn pushed a copy of a London daily paper across the desk to Sara. It was open at the Personal column and one item was marked with a cross.

She read, 'Would Mrs Sara Knight, widow of Timothy Knight, who died in Mexico in March last, kindly contact Bryant and Bryant, Solicitors, of Poole, Dorset at the first possible moment on a matter of urgency.' There followed an address and telephone number.

Sara looked over the desk at Miss Glyn and felt her lips begin to tremble. 'I'd rather not go,' she said. 'I would much prefer not to have any dealings at all with my—my late husband's family.'

The headmistress was regarding her closely and she felt like a fourth-former, hauled before the dreaded presence for some youthful misdemeanour. Miss Glyn was an authority figure—always had been, to all the girls. Fair, but awesome. 'I think you must go,' she said now firmly. 'You have responsibilities, you know, Sara, and you are a grown-up married woman now. Of course, I don't know any of the circumstances, but this is a message you can't possibly just ignore.'

The words of Dr McNab at the hospital in Mexico City came into Sara's head. *Don't let yourself be crushed.* But she had no weapon of independence against Miss Glyn. This was an old-fashioned school. Obedience was a built-in response here, as automatic as cleaning your teeth at night before you went to bed.

Sara nodded. 'Yes, I suppose I ought to go.'

Miss Glyn looked gratified. 'I'm driving into Poole this morning. I'll take you there myself. Let's see if we can make an appointment for you.' She reached for the newspapers and drew the telephone before her. Sara watched her with a horrible feeling that she had been caught in a trap and the door was slowly closing.

But an hour later, when Miss Glyn dropped her outside the solicitor's office in a side road off the main street in Poole, she had managed to boost up a little of her confidence. She wasn't going to meet Jason, she was only going to see this solicitor. Jason wouldn't want to see her any more than she wanted to see him, and everything could be done through Mr Bryant. It shouldn't take long to tell him that she wanted nothing from Tim's estate.

'You'll find your own way back, Sara?' Miss Glyn's gloved hand was on the gear lever. 'I must move on, I can't park here.'

Sara thanked her and pushed open the glass door. The girl sitting at the reception desk had a frizzy hair-do and little beady eyes.

Sara said, 'I'm Mrs Knight. I have an appointment with Mr Bryant.'

The beady eyes surveyed her curiously. And well they might, Sara thought. In these clothes she could hardly

look like Mrs anything. She was still wearing the grey
flannel skirt and white buttoned-up blouse, covered by a
warm grey cardigan, having rejected the idea of driving
with Miss Glyn in the coral trouser suit. Miss Glyn had
conservative ideas about clothes.

'Please sit down—er—Mrs Knight. I'll let Mr Bryant
know you're here.'

Sara sat down on a velvet bench seat in the window,
breathing a little easier. She hadn't really expected Jason
to appear and turn that icy, contemptuous look on her,
but she couldn't forget that Poole wasn't all that large
and his boatyard couldn't be so very far away.

An intercom buzzed. 'Mr Bryant will see you now, will
you please come upstairs.' Frizzyhead led the way round
a corner, up a back staircase, along a narrow passage and
held open the door of an office. 'Mrs Knight, Mr Bryant.'

Mr Bryant senior came forward, extending a hand to
her. He was a small, rotund man, balding and kindly-
looking. He concealed his surprise at the sight of Sara in
her school uniform only slightly more successfully than
Frizzyhead had done, but he settled Sara courteously
into a chair opposite him as if she had been a widow of
mature years and not a slip of a schoolgirl.

'Very good of you to come all this way from London,
Mrs Knight. But perhaps you are staying with the
family?'

'No,' Sara said cautiously. 'But I thought—wasn't the
advertisement put in at Mr J-Jason Knight's suggestion?' She stumbled over saying his name.

'Oh no, I haven't seen Mr Knight for several weeks,
not since he came home from Mexico. I telephoned him
for your address, but he was unable to give it to me. He
merely said he understood that you were in London.'

Yes, of course he would. Aunt Vera thought she was

going to London to join Ralph, and when Sara had telephoned her the day she had left, to say she had arrived safely, nothing had been said to correct that impression.

Mr Bryant coughed. 'May I offer you my very sincere condolences, Mrs Knight?' he said in a professional voice, and Sara blinked and thanked him.

There was a short pause and she knew a sense of relief. Jason hadn't asked the solicitors to find her—he hadn't set a trap—he didn't know she was here.

'Now then.' Mr Bryant opened a large buff folder marked in heavy lettering, 'Estate of Timothy Knight, dec'd'. 'There are various matters we have to go over with you before we can proceed to deal with the administration of the estate. This may all sound somewhat official, but please ask me if you don't understand any point that I may mention.'

Sara didn't understand any of it. At Mr Bryant's request she gave him her birth certificate and her marriage certificate, both of which she had been keeping safely in her handbag, and then she almost ceased to listen. Words like 'intestate' and 'letters of administration' and 'personal chattels' floated into her head and out again. When this had been going on for some time she broke in with, 'Mr Bryant—please.'

He looked up from his papers.

'I really don't understand any of this, Mr Bryant,' said Sara, putting a hand to her forehead. 'And I don't think I would, however much you explained.' She smiled feebly. 'I don't think I've got that kind of brain. I think it would be much better if you just fixed everything up without me. You see, I don't want to accept any of my—my late husband's mony. In fact, I'm quite determined not to. I'll just sign anything you want me to and—and then please may I go?'

It was obvious that Mr Bryant's legal mind was outraged. 'But—but even when everything is shared out, Mrs Knight, you will be entitled to a very large sum of money—very large indeed,' he added reverently.

Sara stood up. 'I don't want a penny of it,' she said, hearing the firmness in her own voice with satisfaction. Dr McNab would have been proud of her.

Mr Bryant was muttering something about '—the shock' and '—only to be expected,' and evidently he had decided to humour her. He asked for her address and she gave him the school address because it was all she had.

'I shall have to ask you to call again,' he said, opening the door of his office, and Sara said,

'Couldn't it all be done by post?'

He was still muttering as he led the way down the dark, narrow staircase. 'I'll see what I can do, Mrs Knight, but really——' He waited for her at the bottom of the stairs and they turned the corner into the lobby together.

Leaning on the reception counter chatting amiably to Frizzyhead stood Jason. He wore working clothes, trousers tucked into short rubber boots, a thick blue shirt open at the neck. With his large bulk and his brown skin he looked magnificent and seemed to fill the small lobby with his masculine presence. Frizzyhead was gazing at him, entranced.

Mr Bryant greeted him fussily. 'Mr Knight—they didn't tell me you were here—would you care to——' he glanced towards the staircase.

Jason replied without taking his eyes off Sara. 'Thank you, no, not now, Mr Bryant. I'll ring and make an appointment later. Come along, Sara, you and I have something to talk over.'

Sara didn't move. In her worst moments she hadn't

imagined it would be like this if she saw him again : her
heart thudding as if it would burst, her skin clammy,
her knees like jelly. If he hadn't grasped her firmly
by the arm she could never have reached the door.

Outside, the feel of the breeze off the sea was like
getting under a cool shower. She gulped in a deep
breath and shook off Jason's hand. 'Please don't touch
me,' she said.

They stood eyeing each other outside the office door
and Sara began to feel her control coming back, and
with it her anger. 'So,' she said, 'it *was* a trap. Mr
Bryant told me you wouldn't be here.'

His mouth pulled ironically. 'Mr Bryant evidently
doesn't know how simple it is to bribe his receptionist.
Wonderful what a silk scarf will do!'

'I think you're disgusting!' She saw the way her face
went grim and a muscle flicked in his cheek and she
had a sense of triumph that she could hold her own, that
she could touch him on the raw.

'Where have you parked your stepfather?' He looked
up and down the street. 'I take it he's with you?'

'Then you take it wrong,' she snapped.

'Where is he, then?'

'I don't know where he is. Should I?'

He let that go, his eyes raking over her grey skirt
and cardigan, with the buttoned-up white blouse. 'And
why are you wearing that ridiculous fancy dress?'

She glared furiously at him. 'If all you want to do is
ask questions that I've no intention of answering I may
as well be on my way.' She turned in what she hoped
was the direction of the bus station.

With three long strides he was in front of her, barring
her path, and, short of fighting with him in the middle
of a busy pavement, there was nothing she could do but
stop.

He stood before her, large and dark and infinitely tough and menacing. 'You're not going anywhere until we've talked.'

She shrugged contemptuously. 'You'd make a hit in a bad gangster film! All right then, let's get it over, but I warn you——'

'My car's just round the corner. Come on.'

She sat rigid beside him in the car, not noticing where he was taking her, and when they stopped she found they were on the waterfront. Jason came round and opened her door. 'There's something I'd like your opinion about,' he said, taking her hand and leading her towards a flight of stone steps in the harbour wall and into a little dinghy that was tied up at the bottom.

'What *is* this?' she demanded as he unshipped the oars and began to row out into the harbour. 'A kidnapping? It won't be worth your while, I've nothing to pay a ransom with.'

His eyes were narrowed against the glitter of sunshine off the water. 'That's what you think,' he said, and she felt a sudden surge of fear—or excitement—or both. She watched his arms, brown and muscular, as he pulled on the oars and a wild elation took hold of her. She didn't know what was going to happen and she didn't care. All that mattered was that Jason was here with her and she could look up and see the grim, dark face with its tousle of near-black hair and the strange, clay-coloured eyes that had always exerted a kind of magnetic fascination over her.

'Are we going out to a boat?' she asked, over the splash of the oars and the screeching of seagulls.

'Where else?' replied Jason tightly. 'I'm a boat man.'

There were dozens of boats of all sizes moored in the harbour, swinging gently at anchor, and as they got near to a pale blue one Sara made out the name *Diana* on the shiny hull. Oh no! she thought. Not Oliver's boat—he's not taking me there! But Jason rowed steadily past without a glance in *Diana*'s direction, to pull in eventually beside another yacht, just as new and glossy but much bigger and as white as a seagull, with a deep blue trim round the hull.

'Welcome aboard,' he said, and climbed up, to hold down a hand to her.

Sara stood on the deck a moment or two later, getting her breath back, looking around. Then, 'I'm very impressed,' she said quietly. 'You built her?' She could have raved about this boat, it was so beautiful, only this wasn't the time for raving.

His voice was quiet too. 'I'm glad you like her, she's my baby. A forty-foot baby.' He smiled. 'Let's go down to the cabin.'

She followed him down to a square, luxurious cabin. 'It's much grander than Oliver's,' she said.

He was still smiling. 'Ah, but you see this was designed and built for my own use and I always make sure I have the best of everything.'

Something in his voice was making her shake inside. 'And can you always be sure of getting the best?'

'Until now I was sure,' he said. 'But now I'm not.'

She avoided his eyes and crossed over to look through the glass above the wooden panelling, and the green water and the boats and the line of the quay beyond blurred before her. Jason came up behind her and put both hands on her shoulders, turning her round and pushing her down into the softness of the velvet-covered bed.

'As I said, we've got to talk, Sara.' He looked down moodily at her, then he turned away and stood staring out of the window on the other side of the cabin. 'I can't expect you to be interested in the story of my life, it's not particularly interesting. Things seemed to be going pretty smoothly for me. I was doing work I loved and the business was going well and the new idea of exporting was stimulating and I was sure I could make a success of it. I congratulated myself I'd kept out of serious involvement with any particular girl. I must have been a smug devil. I despised men who made nasty emotional messes of their lives.'

He turned and stared down at her across the cabin, under thick straight brows. 'I had it all coming to me, hadn't I? That day in Acapulco it hit me all at once. When you threw that cheque in my face I looked at you and I wanted you as I've never wanted any woman.'

Her eyes widened and the naked message in his face brought the heat beating into her cheeks. He went on watching her intently as he spoke.

'After that—well, I don't have to go over all that happened. I think the fiends must have been waiting for me—all ready to strike at once. Jealousy, anger, grief, guilt, lust.' He laughed harshly and ran a desperate hand through his hair. 'God, it sounds like a catalogue of the seven deadly sins! These last weeks I've worked through the lot. I've tried to argue with myself, to use reason, but it hasn't helped. The same answer comes out every time.' He gazed deeply, sombrely at her across the small cabin. 'I love you, Sara, and I want you—to cherish for the rest of our lives.' Suddenly his dark face was shadowed with pain. 'I've behaved like a bastard to you, have I done damage beyond repair?' His mouth softened, grew tender. 'You're such a child.'

Joy was leaping in her, floating through her whole body in great waves. Joy and an almost unbearable excitement.

Her eyes fell before his and she gulped and murmured,

'Correction—I *was* such a child. That night in Cancún you taught me how it feels to be a woman.'

She hardly knew that she had held out her arms, but the next moment she was enclosed and held against him as he slipped down to the bed beside her. Her cheek felt wet as he pressed his own hard cheek against it. 'Are you crying or am I?' she whispered shakily.

'Me, I expect, if there's any justice in the world.' He turned his head and looked deep into her eyes, holding her face between his hands. 'My God, I didn't expect this, I thought you hated me.'

'I worked hard on it,' she admitted, 'but it never really took.'

She watched his face come nearer, then her eyes closed as his mouth took hers, her lips parting to his kiss. Her hands went round his neck, burying themselves in the dark hair as his kiss deepened and became more demanding.

He pulled her down with him on to the velvet of the bed, his hands wrenching at the buttons of the white blouse. 'Does it matter if I tear this damned thing?' he asked, his voice rough and urgent, and she laughed and put her hands on his, helping him.

'God, you're lovely—lovely——' he groaned as his mouth moved down the soft skin of her throat to her swelling breasts. 'You know what you're doing to me, Sara?'

'Yes, oh yes!' She was weak with longing as she pressed against him, her body helpless to resist his hands as they moved over it, awakening new tingling ecstasy every moment. She wanted it never to end, and when Jason drew away at last the tears stung at the back of her eyes.

He stood up and straightened his blue shirt, looking down at her ruefully. 'I mustn't frighten you again,' he said, and she smiled secretly, knowing that nothing he could ever do or say would frighten her now.

'Fasten that blouse up and let's go on deck,' he said.

On deck the cool clean air blew against their hot cheeks. Jason's arm went round her as they looked out beyond the wide expanse of the marina towards the open sea. She could feel his heart beating heavily still, and her own pulses rising to meet it.

For a long time neither spoke. Then Jason said, 'God, that was a close-run thing. You've got such a tempting, beautiful body, my love.' Suddenly he laughed. 'But I make a point of never seducing beautiful young maidens in the cabin of my boat.'

'Jason?' She darted a questioning look at him, but he laughed again and said,

'Bear with me, Sara, I'm having one hell of a fight not to carry you back down there and tear you to pieces with my bare teeth.' His eyes loved her. 'All the same, we might consider having our honeymoon on board—what do you say?'

'Paradise,' she breathed dreamily. And then, rousing herself, 'But we never finished that talk, did we? Do you still think I went off with Ralph, that night he turned up?'

He grinned. 'Ralph wouldn't be seen dead with you in that get-up! So my common sense, feeble though it feels at this moment, tells me that you didn't. Perhaps some time you might inform me where you *did* go.'

'And do you still believe I'm after all that lovely loot that you kept on talking about?'

His hands went round her throat, squeezing it gently. 'Once upon a time, in a former existence, I fancied myself as a hard-headed, cynical type, but not any more. You tell me something—I believe it. If we come across your horrible stepfather again we'll take him on a cruise and push him overboard. And as for the loot—if there's any difficulty about that Dr Barnardo's can have it.'

Suddenly his face was serious, and the strange, clay-coloured eyes that she had thought so hard were shining with tenderness. He picked up her left hand. She had replaced her wedding ring for the visit to the solicitor and the new gold shone brightly in the sunshine. Jason rubbed her fingers against his cheek and then kissed them.

'Tim would have been glad,' he said quietly. 'He liked people to be happy, he was a happy person himself.'

'Yes,' said Sara, her great violet eyes cloudy.

She slipped back into the circle of his arms and he held her close as they looked silently across the sparkling water towards the future.

# Harlequin Romances

The books that let you escape
into the wonderful world of romance!
Trips to exotic places…interesting
plots…meeting memorable people…
the excitement of love…. These are
integral parts of Harlequin Romances –
the heartwarming novels read by
women everywhere.

Many early issues are now available.
Choose from this great selection!

# Choose from this list of Harlequin Romance editions.*

*Some of these book were originally published under different titles.